Summer Haze

At Home in Pennsylvania Amish Country 3

Karen Anna Vogel

Lamb Books

He restores my soul

Summer Haze: At Home in Pennsylvania Amish County

© 2018 by Karen Anna Vogel

Contact the author on Facebook at: www.facebook.com/VogelReaders

Learn more the author at: www.karenannavogel.com

Visit her blog, Amish Crossings, at www.karenannavogel.blogspot.com

ISBN-13: 978-0692187111 (Lamb Books)

ISBN-10: 0692187111

Dedicated to farmers, Amish & English alike, who are sacrificing for each other during severe droughts across America. Your hay relief efforts go the extra mile to help a neighbor. You inspired this book.

.

Table of Contents

Karen Anna Vogel

Amish – English Dictionary

How Pennsylvania Dutch overflows into Western Pennsylvanian slang.

"To be" or not to be, that is the question. Folks in Western PA, along with local Amish, do not use "to be". It's not "The car needs *to be* washed." We simply say, "The car needs washed." This is only one example. This book is full of similar "grammar errors" but tries to be authentic to how people talk in our "neck of the woods."

Ach – oh

Boppli – baby

Bopplin -babies

Daed - dad

Danki – thank you

Dawdyhaus – a small house built for grandparents

Dochder -daughter

Ferhoodled – Messed up, confusing

Gmay – community or church

Groosseldre - Grandparents

Grossdaddi - grandfather

Grosskinner - grandchildren

Grossmammi - grandmother

Gut – good

Jah - yes

Kapp- cap; Amish women's head covering

Kinner – children

Mamm – mom

Nee- no

Ordnung - A set of rules for Amish, Old Order Mennonites and Conservative Mennonites. Ordnung is the German word for order, discipline, rule, arrangement, organization, or system.

Rumspringa – running around years, starting at sixteen, when Amish youth experience the outsiders' way of life before joining the church.

Wunderbar – wonderful

Yinz – You all or you two, slang found in Western Pennsylvania among the Amish and those who speak Pittsburghese.

Chapter 1

The morning air held the scent of lilacs, the aroma calming me a tad. Just a tad. As I searched my *mamm's* careworn face, she avoided my stare and fidgeted with the corner of her black apron. *Was this my stepfather's idea?* I wanted to cry out but bit my tongue. "Why?" was all I could whisper. My throat constricted, but I asked, "Are you following Jeremiah? *Daed* would never leave the Amish."

Shock registered on Mary Miller's face. "We talked it all out."

My real flesh and blood *daed* was still ever-present in my mind even though he passed several years ago. *Mamm* and Jeremiah had spunky twins. Didn't they want to instill Amish values into them? "*Mamm*, will you be taking just the little ones and leaving us baptized ones to run the store? What plans have you made?"

"Charity is leaving with us. We haven't told Shalom

yet."

I felt the adrenaline rush through my veins and I jumped off the swing "What?"

Mary's dark brown eyes were pleading. "We figured you would, too. It's my prayer, Joy."

I shook my head. "And *Grossmammi* and *Grossdaddi?* What about them?" I shouted, pointing towards the *dawdyhaus.* "They've been Amish their whole lives?"

Eyes wide, Mary hesitated, but then sat erect. "They're leaving, too."

Pacing the porch, I kept shaking my head. Was this a nightmare?

"Joy, I truly hope you'll pray about this. We've all had doubts about being Amish for years now, ever since we took a vacation to Punxsutawney and stayed in that Amish B&B. Met all those pastors from the Church of the Brethren. We have much in common except the Brethren denomination drive cars."

The Brethren didn't dress plain, live off the grid, among a host of other differences. *Mamm* knew this. " We all miss Aunt Abigail, but we trust it was God's time to take her."

Mary's face contorted, her eyes wild. With clenched

fists, she shook one towards heaven. "God didn't take Abigail. The Amish did!"

Her words knocked me back. "*Mamm*, are you ill? I've never seen you act like this."

Mary beat her chest. "I've locked up my grief, my rage, and it's taken a toll. I've kept it all bottled up. Nightmares, insomnia, shaking while driving the buggy. Jeremiah made a doctor's appointment last month when it all crashed in, and, it's been a long recovery. You understand, don't you? You'll leave with your family?"

All month *mamm* wasn't sick with the flu she couldn't shake, but sick from grief? I wanted to hug her, but was too numb. Of course, she missed her sister. Dear Aunt Abigail, killed in a buggy accident a little over a year ago. But ask me to leave the Amish? On the day David proposed?

~*~

That night as I paced back and forth across the large braided rug, my twin, Charity, meekly entered the room. "Joy, have you prayed? Will you leave with us?"

My jaw stiffened. "How can you, Charity? We made a vow to be Amish?"

Charity crossed the room and plopped down on her

3

bed. "*Daed* always said you were the most Amish in your ways. He favored you for it. Who else memorizes *Rules of a Godly Life?*"

"David and I did it together," I snapped. "You know we're courting, and I hope to marry him. Wanted to tell *Mamm* today but couldn't." I covered my face with my hands, wanting to block out the world.

"Maybe David will leave," Charity said hopefully. "We know other Amish are teetering."

My legs became mush, and I held on to my dresser. "David?"

"I don't know for sure, but I pray he does. Joy, haven't we lost enough to the Amish backward ways? Cousin Raymond being kicked by his horse while plowing, Aunt Abigail in a buggy. Both deaths could have been avoided."

I yanked open the desk drawer and lifted a copy of the *Sugar Hollow Gazette*. I riffled through it until I got to the obituary section. Scanning it, I named off all reasons for death: cancer, heart attack, car accident. I near spit out "Car accident", anger bubbling up.

"Calm down," Charity said. "I've thought long about this myself, but I think it's time to confess who my special fellow is. It'll help you understand why I'm leaving the

People."

I shielded my face to withstand a blow. "No, not today. Enough surprises." I hadn't cried yet about all that was revealed today until now. I crumbled onto my bed and sobbed like one of my wee sisters. Charity was soon soothing me, holding me close. And then after a spell, she rocked me as she sang the *Loblied*. For twenty minutes I listened as this second song sung in an Amish church meeting wafted around the room. Was Charity having second thoughts? Was she as devastated as me?

My body relaxed, the tension in my neck easing. "*Danki*. Now, if someone special has proposed, which I think he has, you can tell me. It's Jacob Miller, *jah*? You won't leave the People, but marry him? I see how he stares at you."

Charity grew rigid. "You didn't hear me before. I said me leaving has something to do with my beau. It's someone we see in the store every Monday, Wednesday, and Friday."

"Stop!" I jumped up as if seeing a snake. "Paul?" I hit my head, feeling so stupid. "Don't tell me it's Paul Berkley. *Ach*, Charity, the way he flirts with you is nauseating. Do you know he thought I was you? The charm he put on was thicker than a tub of icing."

Charity was a statue, unable to move.

I wondered why *Mamm* said she wanted to be Brethren. Paul's family attended their local church branch. *Ach,* why did we go to that B&B? Run by Amish, but filled that week with Brethren. I shook, and this scared me. Such trembling I'd never experienced. I turned and shoved the papers back into my desk. Was I having a heart attack? Would my name be in the obituary soon? 'Amish woman dies of a heart attack brought on by shock!'

Needing to act, I decided right then to contact Naomi Yoder in Punxsutawney and tell her how my family was swayed by folks who came to her B&B. "I'm contacting Naomi Yoder to get advice. Her B&B is now Amish or trusted English friends only. That's where all this started with wanting to turn Brethren."

"Holmes County has so many varieties of Anabaptist groups, if people wanted to leave, they only need to drive down the road," Charity informed.

I disagreed. Naomi had Ex-Amish at her place, too. And she did it in secret. Through the Amish grapevine, things had changed, and Naomi gained wisdom in keeping unity. What did she learn?

~*~

The next morning Jeremiah asked me to open the store early with him, mentioning something about needing to take inventory, but I knew he wanted to have a talk. He was a reserved man and wouldn't ask me to sit on the porch and chat. We had clipboards in hand, marking off items we lacked. I really was fond of my stepfather, even though I tried to chase him away from *Mamm* when I met him at fourteen. Tall and handsome with his ruddy hair, I knew once he courted my *mamm*, she'd say yes. After saying she'd never remarry, thinking she was too old to have *kinner*, but Jeremiah married her anyway. A staunch bachelor, five years my *mamm's* junior. It was a miracle they had the twins within their first year of marriage. *Mamm's* second set of twins!

His clear, azure eyes had an apology written in them before he said it. "I'm sorry, Joy. I hear you're mighty upset about us leaving the People. I thought we left a few hints, avoiding some Amish rules set down in the *Ordnung*." He raked his fingers through his beard. "Didn't you notice I trimmed my beard and am letting a mustache grow?"

His facial hair was strawberry blonde, and it wasn't noticeable. "*Nee*."

7

"Hard to grow facial hair." He twisted his mouth up as if embarrassed. "We all went to the funeral at Sugar Hollow *Brethren* Church. You weren't surprised we had people from that flock over for dinner?"

I squinted, trying to put this puzzle together. "We attend funerals of Englishers and can have meals with trusted English friends." I sighed. "I didn't know about Charity and Paul. Charity keeping that a secret hurt. I feel deceived. Does Shalom know?"

He raised a hand. "Wait. It's important to me that you don't feel deceived. Your *mamm* and I didn't know about Paul and Charity. He delivers orders to the store and I suppose they like each other."

I rolled my eyes. "He's a domineering flirt. Jeremiah, you can't let her marry him."

"She's a grown woman. Can't hold her back." He fidgeted with his pen. "Joy, your *mamm's* been in bad shape, like she told you. She was the strong one when Abigail died, and never grieved. She found great peace by talking to Pastor Gabe at Grief Share over at Sugar Hollow Brethren. Well, we both see…a faith that's more real over at their church. Didn't you notice it at the funeral?"

"*Nee*, it shocked me. Guitars in church?"

"David played the harp," Jeremiah said so humbly my heart melted. He was too kind.

"I like the silent reverence in the Amish church, how we line up and file in, and share a meal. I find comfort in tradition."

Jeremiah's eyes watered. "You're of marrying age, so you're free to make adult decisions. I'll miss you if you remain Amish. We'll be shunned, and I don't know how the bishop would feel about you working in the store."

My stomach twisted. "Can't you leave after my wedding?" *How could my mamm do this?* Amish women dream of their weddings. They fill hope chests with things needed to run a household and family heirlooms. Tears blurred my vision, but I held them in check. My sobbing last night left me only with a headache. "David and I are engaged."

Jeremiah licked his lips. "We were hoping you'd get married in the Brethren church. David's parents would want it that way."

"Why do you say that?"

Jeremiah cracked a few knuckles. "His parents are hoping their *kinner* will leave with them, too."

I threw my arms in the air. "Let me guess. Lily's

perturbed at the bishop again. She's as prickly as a thorn bush, or so emotional, crying on David's shoulder. I don't see how her husband can stand it!"

Jeremiah shot me a frown of disapproval, and then gingerly moved to the next aisle. "I'm sorry, Joy. You've had so much change in your life. Believe me, if we could change our minds, we would, but we need a clear conscience."

My heart warmed one degree. "Jeremiah, you've been a *gut daed*. Can't you see it's *Mamm's* grief over losing Abigail that she's doubting being horse and buggy Amish?"

Jeremiah headed to the store door and swung the sign to 'Open'. "It's more than riding buggies. Let's both be praying we can come to a peaceful solution. This was wrong of us to shock you. You're too old for us to treat you like a *boppli*. Sure hope Shalom takes it better when we talk today."

As his dejected form made its way to the counter, I felt sorry for him. Jeremiah assumed too much.

~*~

David stopped by later in the day to drop off a circle letter, which made it obvious that he wanted to talk. Amish women love running to the mailbox to get their many letters. He chatted with my *mamm* and then asked if we could take a walk to the back meadow. I told him I was headed there to make a phone call from the shanty.

We walked hand in hand when out of sight of seeing eyes, but his grip was too tight. It was as if he was holding on for dear life. "David, what is it?"

He cupped my head against his chest and held me. "My *mamm* said your parents talked to you about them leaving the Amish. My parents are on the same page," he said with exasperation.

I hugged his middle. "I was afraid you'd be telling me you were leaving, too."

"Well, *Mamm* and *Daed* asked me to pray about it, and so I am. Lots of break-offs among the Amish for centuries. We broke off from the Mennonites, *jah*?"

My throat constricted. "You'd leave the Amish?"

"I can't lose my family to the shunning. I agree with the Modern Amish; shunning is too harsh, breaking families apart."

"But it's how we survive! It's like a wedding vow. *Ach*, David, it's all I've known. How could we leave our *Gmay*?"

He rubbed my back to soothe me. "I don't see an easy solution."

I pulled away and faced the handsome man that so many Amish girls vied for. His brown puppy dog eyes always held such serenity, but not today. "I have an idea. All the unrest in my family's spreading, and it all started at the Amish B&B in Punxsutawney. I have the number in my pocket and I'm calling them. Through the grapevine we've heard they made compromises out there to remain Amish. We need their help."

He forced a smile. "The Amish grapevine. Faster than the internet." He plunged his hands into his pockets. "We need to do something. *Jah*, let's call."

I couldn't help but let a smile escape. *Someone is on my side.* We resumed our walk to the phone shanty we shared with our neighbors. We walked through rows of corn, which were mighty high for this time of year. Missing the farm I'd grown up on, now living on two scant acres, I relished this walk. "Corn will be more than knee high by the Fourth of July, *jah*?"

"*Jah*," David agreed. "Hope the rain keeps up. The ground's soaking up the steady rain."

I loved hearing David talk about farming. It was his passion, and he'd inherit ninety acres. I wanted to be a farmer since birth. *Daed* helped me collect eggs when a wee one. How the roosters scared me, and I'd jump up on my *Daed*. And then my heart skipped a beat. Was David's inheritance at risk? Could he inherit from shunned parents? *Nee*. No exchanging of money with people under the ban. Maybe his parents planned on giving him the deed before they left. I shook my head, letting the idea fly out. My mind was letting in *ferhoodled* thoughts.

When we got to the shanty, I pulled the numbers from my pocket and dialed up the B&B. After three rings, a cheerful female voice greeted me.

"Hello, Secret Garden B&B. Naomi speaking."

"Hello, this is Joy Hershberger. We stayed with you two years ago. We're from Sugar Hollow, Ohio."

"I remember you and your family. So sorry to hear about your Aunt Abigail. I think of *yinz* often."

"*Danki*," I said, pausing to collect myself. "Naomi, I'm calling because there's a rift out here in Sugar Hollow. My family wants to leave the Old Order Amish and be Brethren, and it all started at your B&B. We need your help."

There was no reply for a spell, and then sniffles. Crying? "Hello, Naomi? I'm upset. I didn't mean to make you cry."

She cleared her throat. "I'll be out to Sugar Hollow to clear all this up. What's your address?"

David could hear and encouraged me to have her come. "But it's three hours away," I protested. I wanted to say she was elderly, but then reconsidered. She appeared to be in her fifties or sixties, from what I could remember.

"Hello? Hello? Has your call dropped?"

"Dropped? *Ach*, I'm calling from a landline. Do you have a cell phone?"

"*Nee*, I have a landline. But some Amish use cell phones to call. What's your address? Word has it there's a van headed to Holmes County tomorrow and I must make plans mighty quick."

I gave her my address; we needed help!

Chapter 2

Mamm wasn't too happy that Naomi was coming. Actually, that I asked her to intervene. *Mamm* said there was nothing that could make her change her mind, but when the van deposited Naomi on our doorstep the next day, we had a guest room aired out and freshened up. Naomi seemed to have aged a bit but was still her vivacious self.

"Land's sake, you have a big house," she exclaimed.

Jeremiah introduced her to everyone at the table and asked her to take a seat. Naomi was a chipper songbird in a room of gloom. Then Paul came in through the front door as if he owned the place. *Mamm* set out a place for him, and Charity leaned over to whisper, "He asked to be here."

"It's a family matter," I spouted. Paul scooted between us and put a protective arm around Charity. Didn't Charity see his rudeness?

After everyone filled their plates with eggs, bacon,

hash browns, and blackberry pie, Naomi started the conversation. "Well, Joy told me *yinz* were thinking of leaving, having met some Brethren folk at my B&B. I have to say, I feel responsible. Bishop Dan put a stop to us renting to Outsiders and the place isn't fancy anymore. Lots of tears I cried over that wallpaper coming down, but a small price to pay for unity. We had fifteen Amish leave for the Mennonites, you know."

Paul shifted and grabbed Charity's hand. "I'm not Amish."

"I can see that," Naomi said good naturedly. "You look too old to be dressing fancy as if on *Rumspringa*. You and Charity are apparently a couple and you want her to leave the Amish for you?"

His mouth gaped. "Ah, she wants to leave, as do many others."

"Reason being?" Naomi prodded.

Mamm blurted out, "Buggies! I can live with no electricity and all, but the streets here are loaded with tourists and buggies aren't safe." Her chin quivered, and tears welled in her eyes, and she looked down to hide her sorrow.

Naomi rest a hand on *Mamm's*. "I'm sorry about

Abigail. Sisters are special, *jah*?"

"*Jah*."

Naomi slowly closed her eyes. She grabbed a handkerchief from her pocket and wiped perspiration beads that suddenly appeared above her lip. What compassion Naomi possessed. This woman intrigued me.

"I lost my sister to a buggy accident," Naomi said. "It was horrible. Her husband died, too, and my dear nieces were left without parents."

Without a pause, Paul started to go on about 'testing God' with using buggies, and Jeremiah shot him a glare to clamp his mouth. What Charity saw in Paul was a mystery. He lacked compassion, was arrogant, and didn't respect the Amish at all. Didn't he realize Charity was raised Amish and the People's ways were engrained in her heart?"

Naomi frowned at Paul. "I saw lots of people riding bikes on the way here. The van swerved around them. Are they tempting God?"

Paul blushed and said nothing. Naomi put him right in his place. I wanted to clap in applause.

Naomi wiped the tears in her eyes. "My sister's death was sifted through the hands of God. He's big enough to have stopped it. Truth is, the drunk man that hit them was forgiven by the People and he's no longer a drunk, but a believer in Christ. Has a whole new life. God gives beauty for ashes."

No one said anything for a while after Naomi's revelation. Coffee cups were replenished, and then *Mamm* got that angry look she'd possessed since Aunt Abigail died. "Like I said, we have more tourism and more cars. It's not wise to use a buggy anymore."

Naomi was persistent as a bear getting honey from a tree. "Before your sister went to Glory, did you have a problem with buggies? And why turn Brethren when there's Modern Amish here who drive cars? Seems like someone's been persuading you to leave." Her eyes landed on Paul. "God doesn't like division among His people. Sowing seeds of discord is not his way."

Paul opened his mouth, but nothing came out. He knew Naomi was right. *My fondness for this woman was growing by leaps and bounds.*

Naomi leaned forward. "Paul, you want to marry Charity, *jah*? And she'd be shunned and you'd have one heartbroken wife, so you've decided to lure the entire family away from their Amish roots, *jah*?"

Jeremiah groaned. "We've weighed the matter and

considered all things, like the Bible says to do. Three families want to leave, but do it in God's time."

"Three?" I blurted. "Who else?"

Mamm's faint voice said Becky, one of my dearest friends. Becky King? *Ach, Lord, no!*

Naomi stood and squared her shoulders. "You made a vow at baptism. God will never give you the right time to break a vow. Next thing I'll be hearing is that divorce is allowed among the Amish! The sacred vow that keeps a family together."

I wasn't expecting Naomi to be John the Baptist. What did I expect? A meek Amish woman? A quiet woman? This was my doing, so I had to intervene. "Naomi, can I talk to you in private?"

"Things that can't be said in front of *yinz* all?" Naomi said rather frankly.

Charity politely asked what's a *yinz*, and Naomi let out nervous laughter, breaking the tension.

"*Ach*, we don't live far from Pittsburgh and it's part of their dialect. Now, Joy, what did you want to say?"

I gave her a knowing look that this was indeed personal. *Mamm* seemed to read my mind and suggested I take Naomi out this afternoon to see some sites in Sugar

Hollow. She had her own questions about the loss and grief as a sister, and Naomi said they'd talk tonight.

~*~

Naomi said her desire to see tourist sites didn't appeal to her, only a buggy ride out to see Amish quilt shops. *Perfect*. David's *Mamm* owned one. We drove past the fields of corn, wheat, soybeans and Naomi clasped her hands, saying how blessed we were with so much rain. Her husband had a rain gauge and kept a record of precipitation, something he'd done as a kid being raised on a farm.

"Naomi, I heard you get plenty of rain in Western Pennsylvania. More rivers, lakes and waterfall than these parts of Ohio."

She nodded. "We got poured on this past spring causing a flash flood. Three in our *Gmay* were killed." Her eyes watered. "Still recovering. Many still in deep sorrow."

"That's sad," I said. "In a flashflood, do crops wash away, too?"

"*Jah*, all the winter wheat coming up and seeds sown in spring. Trying to get that first cutting of hay's going to be mighty hard, but we'll survive. You learn to adapt to where you live. When I lived in New York, I felt like a fish out of water for sure. After two years, the cold didn't bother me so much."

"You lived in New York?" I asked, slowing the horse as we neared the quilt shop.

Her face instantly was downcast. "Micah and I lived in my deceased sister's house to raise the girls. Becky and Lena, ages fifteen and ten. Lived there five years until Becky married and could look after her younger sister."

I put an arm around Naomi. "You miss your sister still?"

"*Ach*, I'll always miss her. It's not that. Some folks came to my B&B from Falcon Hill and liked the Punxsutawney Amish, being more liberal. They settled not far from me, and the Amish in New York didn't like it. Those two nieces of mine aren't talking and it grieves me deeply."

"I'm sorry," was all I could get out, unusually edgy when we dismounted the buggy. David's *mamm*, Lily, was out beating a rug and she appeared to be having no mercy on it. She spun around to face me, eyes flashing. David was close to this woman and he must have told her about Naomi coming to straighten things out.

"Hello, Lily. Is David around?"

She shielded her eyes from the sun. "He's right out back, watering my kitchen garden."

Naomi, as outgoing as ever, went to Lily Mast and introduced herself, eager to see her quilts. "I quilt, knit, crochet, embroider and love all things with fiber. That feel of yarn. *Ach*, there's nothing like it."

Lily led Naomi into the shop, and I followed, wanting Naomi to mellow out this high-strung woman. "Lily, Naomi is from Punxsutawney. She owns the Secret Garden B&B."

Lily flashed a smile. "You helped us see the light."

Naomi's glare bore through Lily. "We have the so-called light. I did nothing to help any Amish leave to be Mennonite."

"But that's what happened, right? And Our family's leaving to be Brethren."

"Your *whole* family?" I challenged.

"*Jah*, all of us. You are too, from what I hear. You wouldn't shun your whole family, Joy."

"She made a vow," Naomi said evenly. "She's baptized and so are you. If you've seen the light, maybe you need to hold a candle up to the scripture that says a vow is a sacred thing."

"We were deceived, not knowing any other way."

Naomi sat her wiry self in the wooden chair. "Deceived? How so?"

"Well, we were told we had to earn God's approval by good works. All these plain clothes, no modern conveniences, no cars. God doesn't care."

Naomi squared her shoulders, ready for battle. "We dress plain for many reasons, one being economical. We aren't tied to any regular monthly payments, can sew our own clothes, and drive buggies so we don't miss out on conversation. Too many choices clutter our minds."

Lily sat on the bed that displayed the quilts. "Now, that's a thought. Never heard of that. My parents told me God would send me to hell if I left the Amish." Her face reddened. "Makes me angry how afraid I was of God. The Brethren teaching us God is love, died for us, and all the scripture we were denied, I feel so happy and close to God."

Naomi's eyes grew tender. "You never heard these things?" Naomi went to sit next to Lily and took her hand. "I'm sorry. You must have too strict an *Ordnung* to never hear Bible truths."

Lily averted her gaze out the window, changing the

subject. "Too nice to stay indoors today, *jah*? I'm sure you want to enjoy your buggy ride."

I didn't want to speak over my elders, but Naomi was determined to help Lily. "Can Naomi see the quilts?"

Lily shook her head. "This heat makes me *ferhoodled*."

The two started to talk quilt-talk and I slipped out to see David. Faithful David, out watering his *mamm's* garden. The rows of lettuce, spinach, and kale were perfectly straight. Somehow it reminded me of Lily. Would she ever bend?

I snuck up on David, being a tease. "Boo!"

He spun around, but he didn't give me his usual smile. A welcome smile. "Hello, Joy."

So formal. "David, is anything wrong? Are you too hot? Need some lemonade?"

He pulled at his clean-shaven chin. "I see you brought the lady from Pennsylvania to convert *Mamm*."

"Convert? You mean remain true to her Old Order Amish vow."

He shoveled compost from the wheelbarrow to the garden. "Our family had a big talk last night. Hard to talk about. *Mamm's* mighty determined."

It started as a little bubble and then sprang up, but I

clamped my mouth shut before the words came out. He loved his *mamm* more than me. Of course he did. He had to be there for her emotional support, being such a nervous woman. Lily broke under the smallest of circumstances, always leaning on her first-born son to aid her."

He stepped on field stones and stood next to me. "Joy, our family's leaving. *Daed* said so last night."

"Well, today's a new day and Naomi's here. She'll be talking to *Mamm* about running away from her problems tonight."

"Joy, how can you say that? Buggies kill Amish. It's simple to understand."

The David I'd known since a child was a stranger. Would I lose everyone I loved if I remained true to my vow? "David, what about your vow to the People?"

He clenched his jaw and stared at the ground. "*Mamm* and *Daed* made a vow, too. Need to keep it."

The pain in his eyes was unspeakable. "David, what happened? You're not making sense."

He gripped my shoulder, getting dirt on my pink dress. "Please leave for me. I'm leaving for *Mamm*."

"Why, David? Why can't your *mamm* be strong for her family? You're leaving for her? So suddenly?"

He gripped my hand hard and we walked away from the house, out of earshot of the quilt shop. "Joy, my *mamm* made a vow to her parents to leave the ninety acres to me, so we'd always have family in Sugar Hollow. I never knew she vowed."

"What?"

He blinked as if sand was in his eyes. "I won't be able to get the land if I stay Amish. Remember? No exchanging money with shunned Amish?"

I pressed my hands on his chest to steady him. "David, you won't exchange money. It's a gift. You can accept it and stay among the People."

His eyes grew wild and he raked his fingers through his dark brown hair. "It was decided last night that if I don't remain a part of this family, I won't get the land. Joy, it's been my dream to be a farmer all my life!"

My mind could not take this all in. My opinion of Lily took a nose dive. So, they threatened David. Or bribed him.

"So, you'll leave with us?" he begged. "*Mamm's* never been happier, too. That Bible learning makes her not afraid of death. She was taught she'd go straight to hell if she even thought of leaving the Amish. She's a nervous one for a reason. The counselor over at the Brethren Church said she has Obsessive Compulsive Disorder, an anxiety disorder. She's taking medicine and the Amish would never approve."

"You know that's not true, David!" I near screamed, trying to reason with him. But I let him rattle on. The movie that I'd watched while working at the hotel came to mind. Several families left to start a utopian society, but it was destroyed from within. They all had problems. Sin. One member of this society killed someone else due to jealousy. "David, the Amish aren't a utopian society. We have problems. Crimes have been committed. We all know that. But, we'll never find a pure, sinless place until we get to heaven."

David recoiled from me. "You're not hearing what I'm saying, just defending the Amish. He scowled at me and turned to head back to his house. *He's so bitter, Lord. My Mamm's bitter. Everyone leaving is bitter.*

Chapter 3

As much as I wanted David to meet Naomi, he was in no condition. I wasn't either. I couldn't hold back the tears when we rode back to my house. Naomi's sweet disposition comforted my soul. What compassion this rather blunt and outspoken Amish women possessed. Was she the perfect example of love and justice? I needed her advice, so halfway home, when the tears stopped, though my throat was sore, I began.

"Naomi, I wanted you to meet my beau, Lily's son. I snuck out to see him while Lily showed you quilts." I swiped a tear and told her all that David just divulged. I pound my chest. "I not only made a vow, but love Amish ways. David and I walked the land he was to inherit hundreds of times, making plans of where the house would sit, the barn, even the outhouse."

Naomi was quiet for a spell. And then she let out a mournful groan. "In this world we'll have tribulation, *jah*? From what I gathered, Lily wants modern conveniences and wants her son by her side. She's trying to take too much control of her life and not let it unfold naturally.

That movie came into my mind again. Trying to make an ideal, perfect society. It can't exist on this side of heaven. "Seems like everyone leaving has a hurt, and they're blaming the Amish ways for it."

"*Ach*, it goes back to the Garden of Eden. Adam said, 'This woman you gave me, she made me eat the fruit.' It's human nature to blame others for our problems."

I wanted to lean my head on this dear woman's shoulder. "You'd make a *wunderbar gut mamm*."

Naomi hushed me, saying I'd make her blush. "I wasn't able to keep a *boppli* to full term. I have *kinner* in heaven, but not here. God fills the loss. I told you about my nieces who needed a *mamm*, and there's others in our *Gmay* who call me Aunt Naomi. My quiver is full because God's in control, not me."

Such contentment! "I already feel like I can ask you something personal…"

"Go on. Maybe someday you'll call me Aunt Naomi,

too." Her face glowed at the thought.

"David assumes I'll come around to leaving the Amish with him. We made plans to farm the land he'll inherit. What do you think?"

She licked her lips, deep in thought. "Well, it's not right to pressure anyone to go against their conscience. David thinks his *mamm* can't get along without him? She has a husband, *jah*? And other *kinner*?"

"She depends on David a lot."

Naomi snapped two fingers together. "Needs to cut the apron strings. If you married him, he may still put his *mamm* first, and that would cause problems."

The thought never entered my mind, but would I be second fiddle to Lily? The woman was demanding. What if she got the notion to move out west for more land? Or not be content to be Brethren and want to go English? Would her life be a forever battle?

"If he loves you, he won't let you go." Naomi said, patting my shoulder. "Wait a few days and let him calm down. He may be talking out of sheer panic." She clucked her tongue. "Withholding an inheritance. I know it's done among the Amish, all hush hush, gifts given to kids to join church, but it's plain wrong."

I examined the face of this wise woman and our eyes locked. I smiled and it's as if she could read my mind. She nodded, and all was a quiet peace. I wanted to learn from Naomi her secret to peace. It was more than doing lots of fabric arts. No, she held some treasure in her heart. When Naomi talks to my *mamm* tonight, I hope she sees the same thing and will take her advice.

~*~

The next morning before the van arrived to take Naomi back to Pennsylvania, I sat with her on the front porch. "How did it go with my *mamm*? She seems rather irritated this morning."

"Not too *gut*. I thought since we both lost sisters to buggy accidents, she'd change her mind. She's angry at the driver of the car. Needs to forgive him but won't. She also told me about your *daed's* cancer. I'm sorry *yinz* all experienced that."

My *daed* was reduced to a skeleton, but asked us to promise to not blame God. "Naomi, is she blaming God for my *daed's* death?"

"*Jah*, she is. I asked if he got adequate health care and it seems like your *Gmay* did all they could. Paid for a lot of expenses, *jah*? But they wouldn't pay for alternative medicine in Mexico."

"What?" I was an ever-expanding bubble ready to pop. "My *daed* would have to take the train. He didn't want to go."

"Does your *mamm* know that?"

I let my head hang. "Maybe not. I was *Daed's* confidant. But surely *Mamm* knew he was in no condition to take such a train ride. *Ach,* wait. She's been upset since *Daed's* death that the Amish can't fly." Emotion welled up and I hugged Naomi around the neck. "I wish you didn't have to leave."

Naomi embraced me. "Come out for a visit. For a rest. My niece did that after her husband's death. Lena may be able to help you see the benefit of getting away from all you know, what others expect of you, to know your own mind. She's estranged from her sister in New York because of her convictions, but Becky always treated her like a wee *boppli.* Jah, Lena can help you, I'm sure."

Most likely the sisters are estranged because Punxsutawney had an *Ordnung* different from the one in New York. *Too much division among the Amish.* "I'll call you from the shanty after I get permission from my parents. I'd love to visit."

The van pulled up with many Amish women waving to beat the band. Looks like these women had a good vacation. Vacation. That was something Jeremiah never invested in. Too expensive. Did *Mamm* need a vacation to sort her thoughts concerning Aunt Abigail's death? Maybe we could visit Pennsylvania together!

~*~

When breakfast dishes were washed and put away, I poured *Mamm* another cup of coffee. "I got an idea from Naomi." Taking a sip of coffee, I dared continue with mentioning my plan. "Do you know she lived in New York for five years? She said she appreciated what she had in Pennsylvania; got some perspective. *Mamm*, we need a family vacation to appreciate what we have here in Sugar Hollow."

Mamm blinked in disbelief. "We went to Pennsylvania two years back. Made me less satisfied with being Amish."

"*Ach*, we did go to the B&B. But, we only stayed for a week. Before leaving the Amish, don't you think more thought needs to be put into it? How about you and Jeremiah visit your cousin in Indiana for a few weeks? Go to the Shipshewana quilt show?"

"Weeks? Who would do all our responsibilities? Who

would run the store?"

I sat straight as a rod, confidence rising. "We older *kinner* can. I'm sure Charity and Shiloh would agree that you two deserve it."

"Maybe it's you who needs a vacation to think things over…"

Our eyes locked. There was a challenge in her tone. Did she think I'd waffle on my baptismal vows? "No need for a vacation. I've made up my mind."

Mamm took my hand across the table. "*Dochder*, you're the only one who's not willing to leave with their family."

I wanted to scream that if *Daed* was alive, we wouldn't be having this discussion. There may not even be a breaking away, since *Daed* was content and wise. He'd speak reason into the situation. Call it out for what it was. They were all blaming the Amish for their troubles and wanted utopia. Unexpected tears sprang to my eyes. The image of my dear father came rushing in. How he loved to play with his *kinner* on the tire swing, take picnics and fish. But *Mamm* sold the farm when she married Jeremiah, and now we lived on two acres of land behind the store.

Mamm ran around the table and hugged me from behind. "I'm sorry we don't see eye-to-eye."

I cupped her hands with mine. "I miss *Daed*. And the farm."

She sat next to me. "I miss him, too. All those farm animals did cheer me a bit, too. I know your *groosseldre* feels squeezed in the far corner of the land." Her lips formed into a smile. "Jeremiah is worth it all."

"Of course he is," I said. "But, I'm surprised Jeremiah would leave the Amish. Something isn't right."

Plunging her fists into her thin waist, *Mamm* huffed and this was her signal a discussion was over. She'd had enough. I was jolted into a new reality; Jeremiah's house would not be Amish. *Mamm* would make us all sit at the same table as usual. Emptiness enveloped me. I would not have a home. This house would not be an Amish house. Plans for electricity being put in were openly being discussed and the buggy would be sold. What about the horses?

I stared into my coffee. "*Mamm*, how can I live here and be Amish? Have you thought of that?"

"Didn't think I'd have to." She grabbed the broom from the utility room to sweep the floor that I'd just swept. I watched in despair. Her strokes were hard, as if punishing the floor.

"Mamm, a house divided can't stand. Can you spare me in the store?"

Her eyes were wide in terror. "You're leaving?"

I let my eyes drift across this mint colored kitchen I'd found so much solace in. Baking alongside *Mamm* when I was a teenager, rolling pie crust and kneading bread dough. My mind flew to my grandparents. It would be a relief if they were staying true to their Amish roots. It was *Grossmammi* who taught me how to crochet and knit. "*Mamm*, are you sure *Grossmammi* and *Grossdaddi* are leaving for the right reasons? Are they afraid of not having someone to look after them? I could live with them in the *dawdyhaus*, keep the buggy, horses and—"

"They never recovered from Abigail's death."

Could I sink any lower? *Grossmammi* was hospitalized for a mental breakdown after losing her daughter. I would not press *Mamm* any further. I washed my coffee mug and placed it in the cupboard. It was time for me to make arrangements. But how could I live in the same town and shun my dear family?

~*~

Working the cash register at our dry goods store, I chatted with many from my church district and imagined where I would fit in. Surely the bishop would help me make arrangements, but I couldn't counsel with him now since I'd give away the big secret. When David came in, I was so wrung out in despair, I wanted to run into his arms for comfort.

He waited until the store was empty. "Joy, have you decided? What I told you about my *mamm's* anxiety due to strict Amish ways help you see the light?"

"Anxiety happens to others who aren't Amish. We need to trust God."

David huffed. "And you think my *mamm* doesn't have enough faith?"

I leaned on the countertop, feeling lightheaded. "*Nee.* Not at all. We all struggle."

David drew near and gripped my hands. "*Mamm's* always leaned on me more than my *daed*. Never could figure it out. She needs me, Joy. But I can't imagine losing you."

His eyes were speaking volumes. He loved me, but… *But!* That one word that could change the course of my life. "David, my home would not be Amish. I wondered how I could live in a house and shun my parents, but it won't be necessary because I need to leave. We're divided.

There's too much tension. And I'm finding it too heartbreaking to live in Sugar Hollow. Not being able to celebrate Christmas with my family? No birthdays? David, I think I need to move away."

"Leave? You'd leave?" He was incredulous. "Where would you go? How would you make a living?"

I couldn't bring up the obvious, such despair etched on to David's face. Of course, I'd move to an Amish settlement, rent a room, work my way among the People and hope to meet someone and wed. David knew this. It was the Amish way. I could not raise my head to meet the gaze that was boring through me.

He squeezed my shoulders. "There's a new settlement that's Modern Amish thirty miles south. They don't believe in shunning. You could see your family. I could see mine. Please, Joy. Don't go."

I knew about the Modern Amish. Agreed with most of their new rules. No *Rumspringa*, it only led to lots of trouble among the youth. They had Sunday School to learn more about the Bible. But, they allowed telephones in their homes. Real Amish feared telephones would replace visiting face to face. But I made that vow. Was I so afraid of burning in hell fire if I left, as Charity said? *Ach*, my mind was in a swirl!

"I need time, David. I have this overwhelming urge to run away. I know it sounds childish, but maybe it's my mind saying it needs a rest. A vacation. Naomi Yoder was the only person I could talk to about all this. I felt like I'd known her my whole life."

As I said these words, it dawned on me that I'd found my answer. "She invited me out to Pennsylvania. That's where I'll go."

The bell on the door rang, signaling this discussion was at an end.

Chapter 4

Watching the sunset slowly over the horizon, I pondered nature. It moved slowly. Just when the swirls of clouds grew gray as the light grew dim, ever so slowly, all at once, when the earth tipped just at the right angle, vibrant magenta emerged. Right now, all seemed gray. Right now, all seemed like a haze, so unclear. But as sure as the sun rose and set every day, God's promises to be with me had never failed. His love was constant. Jesus Christ, the same yesterday, today and forever.

Yes, it was time to tell my family I was headed east to Pennsylvania. The past week I'd taken walks along green meadows, picked wildflowers and let my mind rest. It was Naomi's advice when I called her in a panic. Rest. Practice solitude. Go out and do those things that make your heart glad. Summer walks had achieved calm.

So, I possessed an uncommon peace that night when I first told Charity and then my *mamm* and Jeremiah my plan. I would be living with Naomi for the summer, helping at her B&B and see if my heart turned in the direction they hoped for, yet I doubted it.

"I think time away from Sugar Hollow will help you appreciate your roots," *Mamm* said, holding back tears.

I wanted to say my roots were being dug up, not of my own doing, but held my tongue.

"Do you need money?" Jeremiah kindly asked, opening his wallet.

"*Nee*, I have savings from the store and a job waiting for me. *Danki*, Jeremiah There is one thing you can do for me, though. Have the twins draw me pictures and I'll send them packages. I'll miss them and they won't understand why I've left."

"*Jah*, sure," Jeremiah said, eyes tender. "They'll miss you. But you need rest."

I dared to speak all that was on my mind. "So do you two. Don't leave until you have absolutely no doubts."

Jeremiah put up a hand. "We are in agreement."

"I know my twin. She's unsettled. Paul's been acting mighty strange."

Mamm spoke up. "Of course we'll have doubts. It's normal. And Paul's a fidgety one."

"*Mamm*, I don't mean to be disrespectful, but I don't agree and I can say Bible verses to make my point, but I've decided to say no more. It's too much to bear."

Mamm seemed annoyed, but Jeremiah got up and embraced me. What comfort. He apologized again for turning my life upside down, and then he said something I'd never heard. *I love you like a dochder.* And he meant it. It was a soothing balm to my soul. I hadn't felt the love of a father in so long, and I didn't think I needed it. But everyone needed a father of some kind, a strong man, to depend on, I suppose. Love for this man overflowed and I choked out that I loved him like a father. Somehow, I knew this was going to be a turning point, but I didn't know how or when.

I went back upstairs, and Charity said she didn't mind if I kept the oil lamp glowing so I could read my letters. She was more tired than usual, but I knew she was upset. Was the charisma of Paul wearing off? Veneer didn't last forever.

I read through a circle letter first, since they were fun. Recipes, knitting patterns, news from settlements across the country. Either too much rain or too little. Pennsylvania was having quite a dry spell. The other letters were all local, most likely invitations to working frolics and such. But when I opened one from David, my heart did a flip flop. Good news or bad? I read:

Joy,

You've avoided me all week. This need for solitude seems immature. It's like you're punishing me. We need to talk. Face facts. Make a plan. I want you to come with me to meet some Modern Amish. They're a more progressive order and we won't be shunned if we join them. It's the perfect plan. My mamm even agrees and isn't upset.

So, meet me at the covered bridge Wednesday and we'll talk. And don't forget, it's the kissing bridge.

David

"Immature?" I grumbled.

Charity stirred and I mashed my lips. Since when was seeking God immature? Did he miss me because of kisses? His tone was demanding. 'Face facts?' What facts? Did he think I'd throw away my baptismal vow like an old dishrag? As for making a plan, he already had one. A siren seemed to ring in my soul, like a bad weather warning.

I picked up my pen and wrote:

David,

In my solitude, I found peace and a settling in my heart. I need time away to seek God further. I'm leaving for Pennsylvania on Wednesday and will be living with Naomi. I have no doubt God will direct my steps.

Joy

I stared at the letter, knowing I was being sarcastic, but it stung that he thought solitude, seeking God, was immature. Jeremiah's embrace and outpouring of love made my resolve firm, while David was pressuring me to go against my conscience.

I folded the letter and slipped it into the envelope. No editing needed.

~*~

As I held on with each sharp turn, the van driver's calm impressed me. I knew we were headed to the foothills of the Allegheny Mountains, but these roads snaking up and down amazed me. What were buggy driving conditions like in Punxsutawney?

I picked up my quilt square and continued to embroider the kitten in red. To feel closer to the little twins, I'd look to the day when I'd give them this quilt for their double bed. My heart lurched when *Mamm* said they'd be seeing me soon and the girls pulled at my luggage, asking me to take them, too. Rarely did they fuss so, and the urge to drop those bags overwhelmed me, but Jeremiah distracted them with bringing in a new kitten. They could keep it in the house with them until I returned. *Mamm* glared at her husband, but Jeremiah had such heart. He would have let all the cats inside if it was up to him.

Jeremiah's tenderness surprised me no end. When we said our good-byes, he gave me the impression that he respected me for holding to my convictions. Was he having second thoughts? My suggestion to give it more time, to be certain, seemed to shake him. So, he wasn't firm in his decision, like I was led to believe.

And Charity. *Ach*, my dear twin. The truth came out last night when her crying woke me up. When she told me, it all became very clear that deception was at play in the Amish leaving the People. If I could postpone my van ride, I'd be talking to that young man. How naïve Paul thought Amish women were. Or, how charming did he think he was? Well, his sin would find him out. And poor Charity. I shivered. She needed to break things off but quick. *Why did I vow not to tell anyone?*

"What are you making?"

I turned to the Old Order Mennonite woman sitting

next to me. We'd exchanged names, but her name eluded me. *Ach,* my nerves were on edge. "It's a quilt I'm making for my little sisters."

"Very even stitches. I can't wait to get home to a quilting frolic. And church."

Church. Yes, the Mennonites didn't meet in homes. "Is it hard paying for a building?"

"Well, I know what you're thinking. I was Amish and the Mennonite ways are confusing to me at times. It's an expense to own a building, but we use it all week not only for services, but my husband is a doctor and he opens the doors for free healthcare." She wiped her brow. "The Amish bishop allows his People to come since they don't exchange money." She smoothed her hair as if it was falling from her small covering that barely hid her little bun. "I'm shunned, you know."

Naomi telling me about the break-off and her B&B being involved, made me wonder if this woman knew her. "I'm going to live at The Secret Garden B&B with Naomi and Micah. Do you know them?"

Her face split into a smile. "We're close friends. My husband lived there for a while when he returned to the area. We caused Naomi and Micah some trouble, but they're gut Christian people who know balance."

"Balance?"

"*Jah*. They follow all the shunning rules. No exchanging money, services, not eating at the same table, but we talk often. Run into them at The Country Store all the time."

"So, you can live in the same town and talk to your family while under the ban?"

"*Jah*." She opened the white pastry box. "Take one." She then turned around to pass the box to other passengers and they said '*Danki* Sarah'. Sarah! This must be the woman who left the Amish with her doctor husband. Word of that spread like wildfire.

When we settled back into a quiet drive, I had to ask. "Sarah, how could you leave the People? You made a vow. I hope you don't think I'm being rude, but I have reasons for asking."

Sarah's countenance sobered. "The Amish and Mennonites are having quite a time, *jah*? Now some are blending to be called Amish Mennonites. I hope the wall dividing us crumbles." She bit into her donut. "Well, I left to marry my Mennonite husband. I see in the Bible a marriage vow is sacred, but not belonging to a particular church denomination."

I felt like cold water was thrown in my face. "Really? But what about making a baptismal vow? Isn't that sacred, too?"

"Do you think Jakob Ammann sinned when he started the Amish? We were all simply called Brethren at one time. It was Jakob Ammann who wouldn't budge on social shunning. There would be no shunning if it wasn't for that man."

Sarah's tone grew harsh as she went on, so I stopped her. "Sarah, you're right. Jakob was the only one who saw the wisdom in making a vow to the People. How could we survive with no vow?"

Sarah pointed up. "God established the church and builds it, not a man. I'm sorry we don't agree on this, but I have anger towards the Amish."

"Because you're under the ban?"

"No. I don't like to keep talking about the past." She glowered. "No one should tell people what kind of medical treatment they can and cannot have. It's overstepping their authority into our personal lives."

Her statement knocked me back. Something horrible must have happened. I took a deep breath. I wanted to defend the Amish. Of course they had a say-so since they paid cash for medical care. And the many agreements with medical facilities to have a flat rate.

"It was nice meeting you," Sarah said, forcing a smile. "We're home, finally. Back home in Punxsy. I don't mean to be quarrelsome. I'm sure Naomi will answer any of your questions about how the Amish and Mennonites live side by side in more harmony since spring."

"This town seems rather small. I'm sure we'll be running into each other, *jah*?" I asked, wanting to leave on a positive note. But the town was small. And where were the tourists? Certainly nothing like Holmes County.

~*~

I fell to pieces once in Naomi's embrace. She led me to a quaint parlor with loveseats facing each other. "This room used to have wallpaper, *jah*?" I wanted to take the attention off me, fearful I'd spill the beans.

She sat next to me. "*Jah*. It's plain now. Joy, you've lost weight and look pale. And now crying. *Ach*, my child. Did something else happen?"

I nodded, swiping a tear. "I'm sorry. I wasn't crying until I saw you."

Naomi took my hand. "I hear that from many of my

so-called nieces and nephews. Call me Aunt Naomi and tell me what ails you."

"I made a vow to my sister not to tell." I gripped her hand. "But it could change everything back home." I buried my face in Aunt Naomi's shoulder and wept. *Why did I promise to keep such a secret? And how could Charity be so naïve?*

"Joy, I admire your loyalty to your sister, but it seems like Charity is hiding something and asking you to keep it quiet. That's not a vow."

I pulled a Kleenex from my apron pocket and faced Naomi. "You're right. She wants me to hide something. But doesn't love cover a multitude of sins, like the Bible says to do?"

Micah peeked into the room. "Joy, *gut* to see you. Hope you get rest here," he said, eyes filled with compassion. "Naomi, the Miller family wants to know if they can stay another night? We're booked, *jah*?"

"*Jah*. Tell them to book two months in advance in summer."

Micah slipped away. I pulled myself together. "You're busy. I'll unpack, and we can talk tomorrow. Maybe things will look better tomorrow."

"Are you sure?" Naomi patted my back, concern etched onto her face.

"*Jah*. I think I've had too much stress over the past few weeks. Brought my embroidery to calm me."

Naomi cupped her cheeks. "You can go with me tomorrow to spinning. A group of women spin wool once a week. Some girls your age I'd like you to get to know. Lots of teens here."

I didn't know whether to cry or laugh. "I'm not a teenager. I'm twenty-one."

Naomi nudged me. "Same thing, *jah*? Young!" She raised her brows. "See those five dents on my forehead? Almost six. A big wrinkle appears every ten years."

She laughed so carefree and tension ran off me. I made the right decision to come to this small town.

Chapter 5

I got up at six to help make breakfast for the dozen guests, had cheerful conversation with Amish from Florida come north to escape the heat, and cleaned the dishes. Naomi asked me to return books to the library, which was within walking distance. I saw through her. I told her walking calmed me when back home. How I'd roam the fields and pick flowers and watch birds. Everything in nature had order and shouted out that God was in control.

But there were no meadows, only sidewalks. The B&B was in town, but I was curious to see the little shops. I walked the five blocks to the library to ask the librarian for help finding the books on Naomi's list. They were all children's books, which I found unusual. Not many children at the B&B.

When we entered the bright, glassed-in children's room, the most adorable Amish twin girls were on their *daed's* lap as he read to them. He looked up to acknowledge us and nod a welcome. They were towheads, all three of them, and what a picture they made.

"I can read to the kids," the librarian said.

"*Nee*, Helen. It's our special time. They grow up fast."

The young librarian with dyed blue hair in patches turned and frowned. She grabbed the five books I needed and led me out, as if we needed to let the father and girls have their sacred time.

"He lost his wife," she whispered. "Best father I've seen. My dad's a jerk."

When we got out of earshot, I told her I had twin sisters back home and my stepfather was very kind. "That's not your experience?" I prodded, hoping to befriend this girl who appeared my age.

She rolled her eyes. "I know I have a pierced eyebrow and nose but stop staring."

"I wasn't. Honestly. You said something about your *daed* and I…"

"You're Amish and think you have all the answers? Man, half of *yinz* I like, but the other half, too holier than thou."

I apologized for meddling and she shrugged. "*Ya*, my dad was a jerk. My stepdad's worse. Kicked me out of the house. If it wasn't for the Mennonites down the street letting me rent a room, I'd be homeless. And some Amish friends help, too. Some are cool. Like Nathan and his kids. His girls draw me pictures. My frig is plastered with them."

She rattled on so, I couldn't keep up. My mind whirled. Unhappy home. Mennonites help her. Amish do, too. And his name is Nathan. I looked back and saw they were still in the children's room. "Do the Amish and Mennonites help Nathan?"

"Well, the single girls help him. They drop off dinners, believing the way to a man's heart is through his stomach. He brings me leftovers all the time. He's a real sweetheart."

I wondered if Helen was sweet on Nathan. I'd have to ask Naomi about Nathan. Did the *Gmay* help him? Who watched his girls when he worked? What did he do? I shook my head. Why should I care? I have enough to concern myself about.

~*~

Naomi placed a hand on her husband's shoulder. "It's only a small garden."

"*Jah*, but we serve fresh greens from this dry patch. When will it rain?" He picked up a handful of dirt and let it sift like sand through his fingers. "This is bad. Need to water today."

"I can do it," I offered. "Where's your sprinkling can and water?"

Naomi took me over to the barrel that caught rainwater from the gutters. "Sorry. We do it by hand. We have gravity fed water to the house, but never use it for the garden. Makes for less pressure to the house. I'll help you." When Micah left for the cooler indoors, Naomi sighed. "He's been fretting so much. Not like his usual happy self. I suppose the men-folk know more about this drought than they let on."

"We have almost too much rain back in Ohio. When was the last time it rained?" I asked, plunging the sprinkler can into the water and giving the lettuce a drink.

"Not sure exactly. Micah measures the rain in a glass. I'll ask him. The rain has come in spurts, but what we need is a daylong soaker. Not a downpour. Those downpours run off the land and create flooding." Naomi's face drooped. "That flashflood we had in early May was tragic. Many are still healing. Takes time."

The sun beat hot against my face and it wasn't even noon. "Is it always this hot in June?"

"It usually feels hotter. It's humid here in

Pennsylvania, but not during this dry spell. Now, Joy, what's on your mind. You came back from the library deep in thought. Did the bronze statue of a groundhog offend you?"

Offend me? "Why would it offend me?"

Naomi swat at the air. "Well, it sure did offend my niece, Becky. Remember when I said my nieces aren't talking? It's over that groundhog in part. Becky's bullheaded husband accused us of worshipping money."

I winced.. "How could he think that?"

"Well, the whole town celebrates Groundhog Day. Amish and English both work on goods to sell and together we make lots of money. But it's more than that. The *Ordnung* in Falcon Hill doesn't allow friendships between Amish and Outsiders. We're allowed, if they're trustworthy."

I thought of Helen and how Nathan gave her left overs. Very friendly. "We have English friends back home. The Amish here seem the same. I met Nathan and his girls this morning at the library. The librarian, Helen, said he brings her leftovers. My heart went out to both of them, really. What does the *Gmay* do for Nathan? How long ago did his wife die?"

Naomi wiped her brow. "Handsome Nathan Good has one well stocked icebox, meals from hopeful single women delivered daily. His wife died two years ago, you know."

"She got in a buggy accident?"

"*Nee*. She had a brain aneurism. Paramedics rushed her to the hospital, but she never made it. Patty's parents were so devastated, they sold their place and moved to Lancaster. Said they couldn't live in the area with so many memories of Patty."

I didn't want to be judgmental, but Nathan's twins needed their grandparents. "Does Nathan have family here?"

"*Nee*. His *daed* has crippling arthritis and they moved to Pinecraft, Florida, to avoid the cold. Nathan and Patty had a very rare courtship. Mostly done with letters and he came and visited a few times." Her face lifted. "Daisy and Violet call me Aunt Naomi. Nathan drops them off here from time to time. I love watching them. They've been talking about their sixth birthday party here at the B&B since spring."

"When's their birthday?"

"November!" Aunt Naomi hooted. "Lots of time to

plan, *jah*? *Ach*, they make me laugh."

Daisy and Violet. Such pretty names for pretty girls. But I'd never heard of such a courtship. David's handsome face emerged. Would letter writing sustain our courtship? Maybe I'd never marry. *Lord, if it be your will, bring David back to me. You say you're closest to those with a broken heart. That's me Be close and help me. Make me strong.*

Naomi came over and took my watering can. "You don't look gut. I can do this."

"*Nee*, I need to earn my keep. Just thinking of David. Miss him so much, but the more I want to be Amish, the more demanding he gets. I've never seen him be so rude."

Naomi took my hand and led me like a child to two Adirondack chairs near the white garden shed. "Does David know about this secret you're keeping that you said will change everything back home?"

I shook my head. "I'm hoping."

"Hoping for what?" Naomi tenderly asked.

"If I tell you, you cannot tell anyone. Can you make that promise?"

"Well, *nee*. What if it's something that needs counsel? I'd at least tell Micah."

I rested my chin in my hands. "I can't tell you then."

~*~

After supper, Naomi drove us to the knitting and spinning circle, as she called it. And I felt suddenly shy. Shame boxed me in somehow. It's as if Charity's secret was mine. Feelings of guilt and condemnation taunted me. I glanced at the dry fields. They needed water. I needed water.

It was two miles to Naomi's niece's house. I was told she was in a dream-like marriage, the second time around being a blessed union. The first husband died, and Lena didn't grieve at all. Was she a heartless creature? Not talking to her sister, either? Did she try? I'm sure during the chit chat the beans would spill.

We pulled up in front of a white clapboard house, but my heart sank when seeing the rose trellis. It was like Lily's. David often brought me rose bouquets. Ever since Lily's bush bloomed, I'd had plenty of roses. I was only fourteen years old when he gave me my first bouquet of roses. *Fourteen.* I hung them in the attic to dry. When they faded, I crumbled up the petals and made a sachet. It was still at the bottom of my hope chest, but it long lost its scent.

A beautiful woman with vivid turquoise eyes, pretty enough to be on the cover of the Amish fiction novels sold at Walmart, ran out, arms stretched open. This must be Lena. On the side porch was a man equally as handsome, and a *boppli* and little boy with eyes like Lena. Picture perfect family.

"Hello, Joy," Lena greeted, coming around to my side of the open buggy.

"Joy, this is Lena, you might have guessed. Joy's been a big help watering my parched little garden, but Lena, your fields are nearly brown." Naomi eyed the area. "Ruth and Timothy's too. I've prayed so hard for rain, but not even a cloud."

Lena turned pensive. "*Jah*, this drought's getting dangerous. Could you imagine if something caught fire? You heard there's no bonfires allowed, *jah*?"

"*Nee*, I did not," Naomi groaned. "Late night bonfires are something tourists like. Well, we'll just have to set out a telescope for astronomy and make homemade ice cream."

Lena patted my hand. "Your first visit to Punxsy?"

"*Nee*." My mouth buttoned up and it was hard for me to talk. *Joy, pull yourself together!* "I came two years ago to the B&B...when it was fancy. Now there's a rift among our People in Ohio. I came here to think awhile."

"*Ach*, Joy, I did the same thing. After my first husband died, I came to rest at the B&B and I can testify that it did me *gut*. Take care of your health, too. I was malnourished and didn't know it. No appetite for anything but pie." She forced a smile. "But God leads. He's faithful."

I picked up my basket of goodies and got out of the buggy. I didn't want scripture promises flung at me. Lena didn't know what it was like to have an entire family leave the Amish, Charity's secret….and David.

Lena took my basket. "I'm going to help you. We comfort others with the same comfort we receive from the Lord, *jah*? Aunt Naomi told me some of your story and I'd be happy to help you if you'd like to confide in me." She covered her mouth. "Am I being too overbearing?"

I wanted to say yes, but said no.

"You see, my best friend lives next door and she's rather frank. She's helped me speak up. Speak my mind. I was timid as a mouse when I first came to Punxsy."

"Really?" I found myself asking. "I don't know if it's the heat, but I feel shy. Guess I'm used to being around my family, especially my twin, Charity."

Lena tilted her head. "Joy, Charity. Did your parents name you after the Fruits of the Spirit?"

"My *bruder's* name is Shalom, meaning peace. It was my *Daed's* idea. My stepfather didn't carry on the tradition."

Lena looked over at her aunt, a bit dazed.

Naomi interjected. "Joy lost her *daed* to cancer several years ago."

The empathy in Lena's eyes was undeniable. Or was it pain? "Lost my *daed* and *mamm* when I was ten. Aunt Naomi and Uncle Micah became like parents. But, I still miss my parents sometime."

"I'm sorry. Naomi told me some of your story," I said, this woman growing on me. I wondered how much older than me she was. She looked mighty young to be on her second marriage with two *kinner*. Envy pierced my heart. When would I have a family? I was twenty-one, and if things didn't work out with David, I may just be an old *maidel*.

Lena waved at two women coming up the road. "That's Ivy and her *dochder*, Rose. Rose will be married come fall. We're already planning her wedding cake."

Now my heart took a dive.

Chapter 6

Not wanting to learn to spin wool, my brain in a haze, I asked Naomi if I could work on the quilt squares and she laughed, saying Rose brought coloring books at times. Rose was a very pretty girl, brown eyes and dark features, yet there was a hint of apprehension as she sat next to me.

"You're so blessed to be living with Naomi. She's like an aunt to me," Rose said, picking up her yarn. "I stayed with her during some trying times."

I felt like I had stones in my mouth, not able to string a sentence together.

"It's going to be okay," Rose said with confidence. "One thing I learned over the past years is even if we get off God's plan, he finds us and leads us back, if we're willing."

My brows furrowed. Charity was far from God's plan. "So, you've wandered from God?"

Rose gazed over at me and then knit rapidly. "Don't

believe everything people say about me."

The sorrow in Rose's tone was undeniable. "I'm sorry. I've heard nothing about you. I'm sure you've heard about my troubles from Naomi by now."

"*Nee*, I haven't. And I'm sorry for being so overly sensitive. I just came back to the Amish, you know. I left at eighteen to go to college. But, this past spring I lost my job and left Pittsburgh to live here again. Thought I'd die living rural, but like I said, I found my way back."

I set my embroidery in my lap, so curious. "Were you shunned?"

"*Nee*, I wasn't baptized, but my parents treated me like I was shunned. Maybe worse. But lots of problems came to the surface and we've all forgiven each other and are moving on."

It was obvious that Rose was hiding quite a bit of her background, so it must have been serious and painful.

"So, what brought you to Punxsy?" Rose asked. "Just a vacation?"

I was at ease enough to share a bit. "My family's leaving the Amish. We came out to Naomi's B&B two years ago and met some Church of the Brethren..." The shock of it all, the wolf in sheep's clothing that Paul was, sunk in, and I wrenched my cloth, nearly tearing it. That need to run won and I ran out of the house crying. There was a hill behind the house and I quickly ascended it, crunching dry dead grass. Everything was dry. I was dry and bone weary. I heard Rose call my name, but I kept running, as did my tears. How could Paul be so deceitful! *Ach*, my poor Charity. Their deception grieved me more than missing David.

Rose was soon beside me. "I ran track at Pitt. Can't outrun me." She took my hand. "Listen, I needed a friend before. I mean *really* in need. Can I help you?"

Help. I needed help. And I needed to confide in someone who didn't know anyone back home.

"If you knew how bizarre these past few months have been, you'd tell me anything, Joy. Nothing shocks me anymore."

I sat in the grass and pulled at the brown-green weeds. Again, I had no words. My grief like a rock on my soul.

"Do you know my half-brother came here this past spring and was hiding cocaine in our house? He's in jail. How's that for starters. Now, tell me something you're embarrassed of."

I didn't understand this girl, so open about private

issues, but she made me feel on equal grounding. Rose didn't have a perfect life, even though she was engaged and planning a wedding. I took a deep breath. "My sister and her beau plan to leave the church altogether after they become Brethren. Paul read books that made him believe there is no God." My heart fluttered and I paused to calm myself. "Charity sings the *Loblied* or hums it, and I think she's mighty torn."

Rose stared at the ground. "Joy, she's being tempted. I questioned my faith when in college. It made me dig deeper into books about apologetics. I can send Charity some."

"Send them to Paul!" I spat. "My sister would never be an atheist if it wasn't for that snake of a man. He's luring her."

"Paul's falling for the big lie. Look at all this beauty God made?" Rose pointed to the distant hills. "Even in drought, the hills always get to me somehow. Shows me God's majesty. I can see why King David wrote, 'I will look to the hills where my strength comes from'. Who can explain a sunrise or sunset?"

I wanted to scream at Rose, my cheeks hot with fury. All this talk would not change Charity.

"Are you mad at me?" Rose asked.

I picked at the grass. "I broke a vow. I promised Charity I wouldn't tell anyone, which was just *ferhoodled*. Now, I don't know whether to tell my parents or David that Paul isn't this perfect saint."

"Who's David?" Rose asked, a tease in her voice.

"He's my beau, but he's leaving, too. I can't marry a man who isn't Amish."

Rose shielded her eyes from the sun. "I could have stayed away from the Amish or easily be Mennonite, but Levi and I came to an agreement. He's Amish and I'm joining the church for him. Now, you know one of my secrets."

I studied Rose's face. She was serious. "Are you in agreement with the *Ordnung* and the *Dordrecht Confession of Faith*?"

Rose's eyes widened. "*Jah*, of course." She laughed. "Joy, I'm glad you're here. You need a vacation. You're so wound up."

My chin shook again. "There's more," I exclaimed as shame engulfed me. "Charity thinks she's pregnant. *Ach*, I hate Paul!"

Rose hugged me. "Joy, that's horrible."

"I know. I shouldn't hate anyone!"

She huffed. "I mean that your sister is pregnant. I'm so sorry."

"Paul's a flirt," I spit out in disgust."

Rose hugged me again and rubbed my back, trying to calm me. It was what Charity did when I was upset. How I missed my sister. My sister before she ever got entangled with Paul.

"Rose, how can you talk so openly about your family? Aren't you…embarrassed. I am."

She grimaced. "Because keeping secrets is what's made my life miserable for too long. When my family's secrets came out, and they were many, the People came by and asked forgiveness for judging us so harshly. Their words were healing."

The air grew heavy and the scent of rain enveloped me. Rose held a palm up. "It's going to rain. I'll tell you more once we get to the house."

~*~

But it was only a fifteen-minute drizzle. The next morning, sun beat down hard on the dry fields and Naomi had me water her kitchen garden again. As I sprinkled the kale, giggling girls made me spin around. *The girls from the library!*

"I'm Daisy."

"I'm Violet."

They held hands and giggled more.

"I'm Joy. Can I ask what's so funny?" Their laughter was contagious, and I couldn't help but chuckle. "Am I watering the plants wrong? Do you want to show me how?"

They shook their heads in unison. Daisy spoke up. "You're wearing pink, the color of bubble gum and some flowers are pink. We asked *Daed* why we can't wear pink and he said 'just because', but maybe you can tell him why and we can wear pink!" Daisy pointed at the house. "He's in there. Please? Tell him why we can wear pink!"

"I can tell you and you tell your *Daed*," I said, feeling oddly shy. But my face must have looked eager because they took me by the hands and lead me into the house. Nathan and Micah were talking at the kitchen table.

Nathan's brow was pinched. "Girls, I need to talk to Micah. Go on outside and play."

Daisy jumped on tip toes. "*Daed*, we have something so important to tell you. Joy has the answer! We can wear pink!" She eyed her sister and the giggling ensued.

Nathan tried not to laugh but he did. "Nice to meet you, Joy." He tilted his head and pursed his lips. "Pink. The problem with pink. Joy, can you explain it?"

Now I couldn't help but see the merriment of pink being the most important issue in life. *Ach,* to be a child again! "Well, girls, I came from a different *Gmay* and we voted on colors allowed by Amish women. I suppose lots of women and their husbands liked pink because they voted for that color, along with other pastel colors. But I see that dark colors are worn here."

Daisy eyed Nathan. "*Daed,* let's have the People vote. Change the colors. *Mamm* loved pink flowers."

All fell silent. The girls loved pink because it was a connection to their *mamm.* "How about I take you to pick wildflowers that are pink?" I offered, seeing Nathan's troubled face.

Violet put her palms up. "I haven't seen pink flowers this year. God's not giving us rain."

I gulped. It was true. "Well, we can plant some nice wax begonia's. I saw some for sale at a greenhouse. We could buy some and then you could have a flower garden. A pink garden." I looked to Nathan for approval and he nodded that I had it. "Girls, come to think of it, there's at least four kinds of pink flowers to buy." I clasped my hands, excited at the prospect, as I loved flowers.

The girls jumped again and giggled. "We'll plant a pink garden and everyone will see pink's the best color," Daisy informed. "And then we can vote to have pink dresses." She hugged me. "I want a dress just like yours."

I knelt and faced them. "But if you can't wear pink, it's still worth having a pink garden, *jah*?"

They bobbed their heads in agreement, blond braids flapping.

Nathan let out a laugh. "It won't stop with a garden. You girls will want me to paint the tire swing pink after that."

Violet gasped. "*Daed*, that's a *gut* idea!"

Daisy grew pensive. "*Daed*, Helen has blue hair. She said she puts blue Kool-Aid in her hair. We have pink Kool-Aid. Can I try it? Helen said it comes out. *Ach*, please *Daed*!"

Nathan looked to me for help. "I love yellow. How many flowers are yellow? Lots. I think God likes yellow. Don't change what God created."

The girls examined their blond braids. After a few seconds, Violet blinked back tears. "*Mamm* loved our hair yellow, Daisy. We shouldn't make it blue."

Daisy shrugged. "Okay, but we'll have a pink garden out in front of the house so everyone can see it and not be so mean to the color pink."

Micah hit his knee and doubled over laughing. "*Jah*, we need to be nice to pink." He elbowed Nathan. "We don't have rain, but you have pure sunshine living in your house day and night. Be thankful and we'll keep praying for rain."

Nathan nodded. "You're right. Worrying about it won't change a thing."

"Well, *gut* planning does. Word has it there's a truckload of first cut hay being delivered from New York. It'll be our first hay relief."

I led the girls outside, asking them to help me water the kitchen garden. Their little ears didn't have to hear talk about the drought. They needed to ponder pink.

~*~

After dinner, Naomi and Micah sipped homemade root beer on the porch. I pulled back the white curtain to study them. Micah seemed to age over the past week. He tried to be cheerful, but his mirth fell flat. Naomi leaned toward him, attentive to him. When Micah seemed to relax,

I decided to join them, wanting to take in the summer breeze and embroider more quilt squares.

"Do you mind if I join you?"

"*Jah*, sure," Micah said, not convincingly. "Made this batch of root beer. In the frig if you'd like some."

"*Danki*. I'm fine."

Naomi tapped the cedar wood chair next to her. "We're just talking about the drought. Amish folk up in Cherry Creek plan to deliver hay by truck next week. It's a great blessing to the Amish who farm for a living."

"Well, that's *gut* news. Why don't you seem pleased? Will it cost too much?" I asked.

Micah and Naomi squinted, as if I were a hard bug to see. Had I said something wrong? Being too nosey?

"No charge," Micah informed. "It's a relief effort."

I shook my head. "Of course. Amish in my neck of the woods have participated. Some rent big semitrucks to take wheat out west. Never had to do it for Pennsylvania, though."

"Well, back in the 1980s we had a drought and a caravan of trucks filled with bales of hay arrived from Lancaster." Naomi picked up one of my quilt squares. "*Gut* work. Even stitches." She bit her lip. "Truth is, my niece

Lena is low. She didn't live in Cherry Creek but Falcon Hill. Not a word from the *Gmay* she grew up in. While others are writing relatives, even articles in The Budget, Lena's heard nothing from her sister."

The hollow in my heart ached again. I didn't want to add to Naomi's sorrow. But, I was hoping for more letters from back home. I was being impatient, perhaps, but I imagined David would write me regularly. When he spent a month away last summer helping a new Amish settlement, he wrote three times a week. I wrote every day.

I scratched my chin. David helped a new Amish settlement last summer but this summer he planned to leave the People? It was all too surreal, and I still doubted any of them would leave when they came to their senses.

Naomi sipped her lemonade. "*Ach*, Joy, I forgot to tell you that your *mamm* called this morning. It was a quick call, less than a minute. She sends her love and says they're well. She's concerned about you, of course."

"What did you tell her?"

"Well, I didn't tell her you fell apart at the spinning group, but that you made a *gut* friend in Rose already. That Rose came back to the Amish after living out in the world, joining church come fall. Your *mamm* seemed to want to end the conversation right quick. Her conscience is bothering her."

I inhaled sweet lavender growing all around the porch, but it didn't calm me. "I suppose an Ex-Amish coming back to the People is the last kind of friend *Mamm* would want me to have. I think she's hoping for me to meet other types of Anabaptists here in Pennsylvania, especially Church of the Brethren."

"I talk on the phone a lot, taking down reservations and whatnot. I can tell by the tone of voice that something's wrong. I think you better call her," Naomi said.

"We only have a phone shanty to make calls. I'll write. Let them know about the drought, too. Maybe they'll pass word along and they can help, too."

"That's a *gut* idea," Micah said as he rose. "I'm heading inside. Feel tired."

After the screen door swung shut, Naomi bit her clenched fist, eyes brimming with tears.

"What is it? Is Micah okay?"

She couldn't speak for a while, only bowing her head as if in silent prayer. Her eyes met mine. "He's pushing sixty, you know. His *grossdaddi* and *daed* had strokes in their sixties and he's convinced he'll have one, too. All the stress over the past several months have taken a toll on him. So many leaving the Amish, us having to make our B&B plain, no fancy wallpaper. He says he's accepted it, but I know he hasn't. Needs some cheering up."

"Daisy and Violet!" I blurted. "Those two can cheer up anyone. Did you hear about our pink garden?"

Naomi's wrinkles smoothed out. "*Jah*, Micah told me. And he really smiled about that."

"So, he can help us. Those girls are so dear. Really is a sad thing that they don't have a *mamm*, but you're like a *mamm* to many, maybe I can be a *mamm* or aunt to them. Darlings is what they are."

Naomi nodded. "They'd be *gut* for you. Nathan would, too."

Shocked by this statement, I sat up like a ramrod. "What? I'm nearly engaged to David."

"I don't know, Joy. I think his *mamm* has great influence over him, even more than the land he'll inherit. And, I've meant to tell you that I admire how you've made a stand, holding fast to your baptismal vow despite your family leaving."

A ruby throated hummingbird took nourishment

from the feeder dangling off the porch rafter. "It's getting harder, I must admit. Reality is sinking in every day that passes and they don't write and tell me that this nightmare is over."

Naomi offered me her hand and I took it. "You're welcome to stay here as long as you want. Maybe you'll settle here. I saw at *Gmay* you turned some heads. Andy Weaver got all bruised up over you."

"What? He fought with someone?"

"*Nee*, he was staring at you and tripped over a sawhorse being set out to make a table and flipped. The men haven't stopped teasing him yet."

I laughed with her as we squeezed hands. "You know my heart belongs to David. He's stronger than you think."

As I sat there, noticing the twilight set in, the sky turning magenta. I hoped David would never change.

Chapter 7

I couldn't fall asleep, the night being too hot and humid. I turned on the little lamp and decided to write to David. Rose was right. It wasn't fair for Charity to make me promise to hide sin. Paul needed to be exposed. I took out paper and a pen from my desk and wrote:

Dear David,

I'm sorry for leaving without saying good-bye. I will explain in this letter how distracted and upset I was and basically ran away to get away from it all.

I know others may see this letter, so I'll be brief. Paul isn't who he appears to be. Charity told me he learned in college that there is no God. No wonder the People don't go to college, teaching such rubbish. He's an atheist and he and Charity plan on leaving the Church of the Brethren after they get married. So, Paul's a wolf in sheep's' clothing.

Charity sings the Loblied so mournfully, I know she's torn right down the middle.

With this new information, I'm asking you to do the right thing. Expose Paul! Your family is being deceived by him.

I need to talk to my Mamm. Can you ask her to be at the phone shanty Friday night at seven o'clock?

I miss you!

Your Joy

PS. There's a bad drought out here. New York had a hay drive. Can you ask the bishop if any aid can be sent here? I'm sure word of the drought has reached Sugar Hollow. Like you always said, the Amish grapevine is faster than the internet.

I reread the letter, itching to tell him of Charity's pregnancy, but decided to confide only in Rose. No one in Pennsylvania knew Charity. And truth be told, it was too painful a topic. I wanted to tell Aunt Naomi, but she knew my family. Would she think I was *ferhoodled* to keep such a secret and not write to my folks back home? I got heartburn just thinking of it, so I pushed it out of my mind. Call it denial, like Rose did, but lately life was easier living as if things hadn't changed. That I'd wake up to find this all to be a very bad dream.

~*~

The next day when I slipped the letter in the mailbox,

I was shocked to see a bouquet of pink flowers held together with a pink ribbon. A pink envelope with 'Joy' written in a child's handwriting made me smile. Ripping open the letter, I read:

Joy,

Do you like pink jello? Do you know pink is in a lot of food? Watermelon, strawberries, and lots of other yummy food. We asked if we could have a pink picnic, and daed said yes! He asked if you'd be there and we said for sure and certain. He smiled real big. Can you come over to our place for the noon meal on Friday? Bring some pink treats?

Daisy and Violet

PS. Hi Joy. The girls were at the library and they asked me to write all this down. I put it in your mailbox along with the flowers.

Helen. PS. I have pink streaked hair so the girls will stop begging me. They don't like blue!

Laughter bubbled within. What a pleasant surprise. I scooped out runaway petals left in the mailbox, placed my letter in, and raised the red flag.

Friday. I'd be talking to my *mamm* on Friday to tell her all I knew. A pink picnic would be a good diversion before that unpleasant task.

I ambled back into the house and found that Aunt Naomi and Uncle Micah were glum. "What is it?" I asked.

Micah let out a sigh. "When Nathan came over, he shared his concern that he couldn't run a farm and watch the girls. Said the strangest thing about sending the girls to Lancaster to be raised by their grandparents." He scratched the back of his neck. "I advised him not to. Naomi and I went to live in Falcon Hill to care for our nieces, but their parents were dead. I don't know why Nathan would consider such a thing."

Naomi clucked her tongue. "The grandparents are pressuring Nathan. They never did think him a capable man. Treated him like he was so backward."

I took a seat at the table. "From what Helen says at the library, he's a *gut daed.*"

Naomi swooshed at the air. "Thelma treated everyone like that. She was from Lancaster, but Bruce from here. Bruce understands hard work, but Thelma just wanted to cater to tourists with her pie business."

"Naomi," Micah quipped. "Why can't the girls stay here until the drought is over? It's really the reason why Nathan's so distracted. Those girls make me laugh."

Naomi gasped. "I have enough to do already." Her

gaze slowly shifted to me. "But truth be told, I've been creating things for Joy to do." She clasped her hands with delight. "Let's invite them here for a week to see how it goes. Nathan may just need a break."

I knew Naomi was struggling to keep me busy. The B&B wasn't a bustling place. With the drought warning across Western Pennsylvania, Amish tourists who came regularly to see the lush green hills were keeping away. And the heat was unbearable in many Amish businesses with no air conditioning. Naomi had wrung her hands over this, and Micah seemed worried. And I fear that I certainly wasn't living up to my name, not being very joyful, but fretting over my private concerns. "I'd love to have the girls here, of course. I can drive over now and invite them."

Naomi threw me a broad smile. "*Danki.*"

Uncle Micah scooped a few runaway pink petals off the table. "Where'd these come from?"

I showed him the letter and he read it out loud. His eyes grew wide. "Nathan smiled real big. Now, I don't see that every day. Joy, I'm not a prophet of God or anything, but I do believe the gut Lord brought you here for a reason." He glanced at Naomi and she pursed her lips, suppressing a smile.

"It's only a pink picnic," I said with a laugh.

~*~

I halted the buggy in front of Nathan's house to soak in the view. The house was situated so pleasantly. The driveway went over a little creek and then to the right of the large white house. The same style as every Amish in Punxsy, with white curtains peeking through, but pink roses climbing on a fence close to the house gave it charm. My heart sank. Daisy and Violet loved pink for a reason. I imagined the girls picking these flowers with their *mamm* and my heart enlarged to take in these two precious ones and bring them joy.

Nathan ran out of the house and yanked at the water pump, dousing his blonde hair. The girls followed like ducklings, but when they wanted to splash in the water, Nathan took the bucket that hung from a nearby hook and let them cool their faces off. "We can't waste water. *Yinz* girls are hot, *jah*? No creek this year?"

They groaned and I felt like I was eavesdropping. I nudged the horse into the driveway, making my presence known. Nathan appeared puzzled and shy but the girls jumped like grasshoppers.

"Did you get our flowers?" Daisy asked.

"*Jah*, I did. *Danki*. I love pink flowers. And I got your notes, too. It's why I stopped by. Can I talk to your *daed* about our pink picnic?"

The clasped each other's hands and ran into the house, giggling.

Nathan seemed defeated. Did he think I was one of the single girls vying for his attention?

"Nathan, you know the B&B is slow right now. Naomi and Micah sent me over with an invitation for the girls to stay for a week at the B&B. It has electricity, you know, and there's fans everywhere. We can plant a pink garden and I think Micah's excited to have a pink picnic. He said he'd make homemade strawberry ice cream."

Nathan's eyes appeared to brighten, but soon dimmed.

"Is something wrong? This was Naomi and Micah's idea, you know. Not mine."

Nathan shook his head as if coming out of a bad dream. "*Ach*, that sounds like something they'd do. I'm sorry if I seem like I'm in a bad mood. I'm not. Just got a letter from Lancaster and their *grossmammi* wants them to come live with them for a while." His chin quivered, and he tried to hide it with his hand. "I never realized that

Naomi and Micah are like kin. They want to help?"

Empathy for this father overwhelmed me. "They asked me to call them Aunt Naomi and Uncle Micah, too. Said it makes their ever-expanding quiver full."

Nathan nodded. "They never could have *kinner* but now they might have too many?" He slid his fingers up and down his suspenders and smiled. "I'll write the *groosseldre* and tell them I have kin here." He picked up the bucket. "Joy, you just made my day."

I was running through fields of pink roses, yet the thorns didn't prick me. Someone was holding my hand and we laughed more the faster we ran. All our cares fell off like a snake sheds its skin. Yes, we were in a large garden like Eden and we were enraptured with joy.

I turned to him and saw Nathan.

I sat up, gasping for air I blinked my eyes to make out my plain Amish room. But the furniture was out of place and Charity's bed was missing.

"What is it?" I heard a voice and a flashlight soon illuminated a familiar face. "Naomi?' I collapsed on the bed. "I'm sorry. Bad dream."

Aunt Naomi sat at the foot of my bed. "You were

laughing."

I pressed my fingers to my cheeks. "I was?"

"*Jah*. Laughing and talking. Doesn't sound like a bad dream."

I was so embarrassed I wanted to burrow under the sheets. "It was a *gut* dream until the end."

"What did you dream?" Naomi prodded.

Curious as to why she asked, I turned a question to her. "What did you hear?"

"Well, a lot about roses and flying…and holding hands. Love."

I brought up my knees and hugged them. "Aunt Naomi, have you ever dreamt about someone else besides your husband?"

The light cast a distorted image of Naomi, making her appear more dramatic than usual. "I don't dream much. But I'd have to say no. I've never dreamt of another man, neither have I considered another one. Micah is mine and I'm a happy woman. Why?"

"I had a *gut* dream about someone, but it wasn't David. Is that wrong?"

She reached for my hand and I took it. "Was it about Nathan?"

Fatigue loosened my tongue. "*Jah*. It was about Nathan."

"Joy, before I was married I had other beaus, believe it or not." She chuckled. "It's ancient history. But I do remember dreaming of men who I courted while engaged to Micah. The dreams were more of a nightmare though. I get up to get married and Roman Klein is the groom. When I woke up, I sure was glad it was a dream."

"My nerves are shot over all that's gone on with my family and David. He seems so far away and hasn't written yet. Is that bad?"

Naomi shifted. "You've been here over three weeks with no letter?"

"*Nee*." Tears pricked my eyes, but I held them in check. "Maybe David is busy trying to make his family see reason."

Naomi licked her lips, scrunching up one side of her face as if pondering something and then said. "The dear Lord above speaks to us by putting impressions on our heart, like a holy nudge. Maybe sometimes a dream."

"What? Holy nudge?" I was too tired to have this discussion, but Naomi was wide awake, so I listened. "Holy nudge. Like a prodding? Like when I met Paul and knew he was a wolf in sheep's clothing?"

Aunt Naomi snapped her fingers. "*Jah*, that's it. Do you know I couldn't stop thinking of my pen pal and so I prayed? We matched up the time I felt led to pray to when she had her miscarriage and it was the same time."

My head was swimming. "So, your prayers didn't work? She lost the baby."

"Emma said she felt great comfort, like the Lord was very close to her broken heart. Since I had so many miscarriages, I was able to empathize more. Comfort her with the comfort I got from God, like the Bible says to do."

I lifted my long hair off my neck, feeling suddenly very hot. "Can you pray for me? I need comfort."

"Of course, you do. I've been praying for you." She cupped my cheeks. "You've been on my heart quite a bit." She leaned to kiss my cheek and softly whispered a good-night.

I laid back in bed and stared at the ceiling. I felt so guilty dreaming of someone other than David. Maybe I was nervous to care for the girls. They'd be arriving tomorrow. Maybe I missed my little sisters. Surely Nathan, as handsome as he was, had nothing whatsoever to do with my dream.

Naomi was such a wise woman. She was the one who told me to seek solitude, talk to God so I could see clearly what to do. And I did. That week I mulled over Isaiah 40:31, the scripture I'd committed to memory: 'They that wait upon the Lord shall renew their strength.' I needed to make these quiet times regular in my life. Maybe like Ruth and Lena's fifteen-minute daily prayer time. Maybe Naomi would do it with me. *Ach,* now I was wide awake!

Chapter 8

Nathan dropped off the twins and we had a fine day planting our pink flower garden, but my dream unsettled me. Seeing him today, my cheeks burnt. Could he see through me? Could I see through myself? I never thought I'd be so fickle, but I kept reminding myself that this was good for me. David had my heart for so long, I never dreamt of a life without him. Until now. But like gold is tried to be pure in the refiner's fire, I supposed my love for David was being refined as well.

As dinner approached, Micah took the twins to the tire swing and Aunt Naomi and I cooked and baked for the guests that had arrived last night. Just when I was rolling out another pie shell, Nathan walked into the kitchen. He took off his straw hat and inhaled. "*Ach*, smells *gut*."

"You can stay for supper," Naomi chirped. "Plenty to go around. Made a strawberry pie for you to take home. It's your favorite and I know it's hard having the girls here."

He took a seat in the Amish rocker in the corner. "*Danki*. I miss them, but it eases my mind that my mother-in-law knows I have kin." He smiled fondly at Naomi. "Were they *gut* today, Joy?"

"*Jah*, very *gut*," I said. "Planted pink flowers and Uncle Micah made strawberry ice cream, which of course is pink." I shifted. "Do the girls like pink because their *mamm* planted all those pink roses?"

He shook his head. "Those roses have been there for twenty-some years. Came with the house, I suppose. But my wife sure loved to pick them with the girls."

Aunt Naomi sighed. "I remember all those mason jars full of flowers. Smelt so *gut* over at your place."

Nathan's countenance drooped. "No time to cut them now."

"We can," I blurted. "If the girls want to pick flowers, I'd be happy to make that tradition continue."

His ocean blue eyes swam with feeling. "I'd appreciate that. I asked Rachel, Mary and Miriam to help the girls pick roses when they drop off meals, but they never showed much interest."

Aunt Naomi chuckled. "That's because their only

interest is *you*."

He raised a hand in protest. "It's the Amish way, to help a widow or widower…"

Aunt Naomi burst into laughter. "You're too modest. Don't you see those girls want to be asked out on a buggy ride, not pick flowers with your girls?"

"You exaggerate."

"Do I?" Aunt Naomi asked. "I can find out."

"*Nee*," he quipped, and then laughed. "I never took you for a matchmaker, but you know I'll stay a bachelor."

"You're not old enough to say such a thing. You married too young and are wet behind the ears yet."

They went on in playful banter and I focused back on my pie shells. I decided to be faithful to David, avoiding temptation. I thought of how David and I met, and then *wunderbar gut* memories fell in rapid succession, like a waterfall. David had never left me insecure about his affections. He loved me more than inheriting land. I'd overreacted once again.

As the dust settled, I could see clearly. Paul would be exposed, and my family would be appalled and stay Amish, along with the other families. Tomorrow I'd be calling my *mamm* at seven. I sure wish I told David to be there so I could talk to him.

~*~

I kept myself unusually busy the next day so it would fly by and I'd be talking to my *mamm*. When the clock struck seven, I dialed up the number for the phone shanty and on the second ring I heard my *mamm's* voice. "Joy is it you?"

"*Jah, Mamm.* How are you?"

"Well, not *gut*. I'm mighty confused. David told us what you thought of Paul, but he denies it. He said his faith has never been stronger. What gave you such notions?"

"Charity," I blurted. "Did you ask her?"

"*Jah.* She said they had doubts but talked to our pastor. It's normal to have doubts at times."

I gulped. "And you believe Paul?"

"*Jah*, I do."

"Does everyone else?" I asked.

"*Jah*, everything's still the same, Joy. We're all in agreement. Have you been able to think out there in Pennsylvania? I'm praying for you, *dochder*. Please, let's all be a family."

Sorrow flooded my heart. "No change, *Mamm*. I couldn't imagine not being plain."

Silence and then I heard sobbing. "I've lost so much to the Amish. Now my *dochder*?"

Mamm's word's stung. I was adding to her sorrow? I thought of my *grossmammi* and her breakdown after Aunt Abigail's death and I feared for *Mamm*.

"Paul and Charity are officially engaged," she said evenly. "I hope you'll come to the wedding, shunning or no shunning."

Nausea washed over me and my legs wobbled. "Charity's engaged? She had doubts about Paul last we talked."

"We all have doubts, like I said. It was being Amish and such strict rules that made us all feel sinful for having one. Joy, I'm sorry I raised you Amish. If only I'd known a better way."

There was no better way, I wanted to scream. If I'd been cooped up on a farm all my life, I might be tempted to explore the Outside world, but working the store, seeing Englishers regularly, I felt sorry for them. They changed like the seasons, trying to fit in or be accepted. They were like Helen's hair colors. "*Mamm*, when will you tell the bishop?"

"This week. Charity's wedding is in a month and she

wants you to be the maid of honor. So, let me be clear. You're my *dochder* before you're Amish. I expect you to love your family more than the Amish. Your *grossmammi* will be crushed if you don't leave."

Shock deemed me speechless. Charity married in a month? Be a maid of honor? *Grossmammi* would teeter on another breakdown if I didn't leave the Amish?

"*Mamm*, what is David going to do?"

Her voice raised a notch. "He's honoring his parents, like the Bible says to do."

I had to sit down. "He said that? You heard him say it?"

"*Jah*, and he's praying for you. We're all praying. Joy, you're sowing seeds of discontent, and it's given me grief."

Aunt Naomi came near me to hold my hand. The room began to swim. "*Mamm*, can we talk tomorrow? This is all too much. I feel ill."

"I'll have David talk sense into you. Call the shanty tomorrow night at seven."

The phone clicked and I just stared at the receiver. Disbelief over all that was revealed grieved me to the core and I cried for some time, while Aunt Naomi lent strength.

~*~

The next morning, I counted three drops of red food coloring and pushed the bowl full of salt and flour dough to Daisy and Violet. "Now, you squish it all up and see what happens."

Uncle Micah watched in wonder as the girls' nimble fingers dug in and worked the dough. After a minute, they squealed in unison. "Pink!"

Daisy had an inquiring mind. "Three drops made all this color?"

Uncle Micah stroked her head. "If Joy put in more you'd have red dough." He scratched his head. "You did say pink, right? All Joy has to do is put a drop of blue in to make purple." He reached for the blue dye and held it above their dough. "You want purple?"

"*Nee!*" Violet slid the bowl to herself. "We like it pink."

The girls had lost their *Mamm* but their spirits weren't crushed. What made children so resilient? The conversation with my *mamm* kept me up half the night. Didn't they see Paul was in a rush to be married? Did they suspect why? Did Charity's pregnancy show?

All this cut me deep, but what speared me was that David was going to call and talk sense into me? This is what kept me up. Reminiscing about my relationship with David. I'd always gone along, letting him lead. There was never a major decision to make that we butt horns on except for once. When we started to court when I was sixteen and said I'd like to get to know a few other fellows in the *Gmay*. How was I to know what men were like if I'd only liked David? Since fourteen folks talked about us getting married someday, but when I was old enough to be taken home from Sunday night singings, I left once with Elias Miller. He'd reached me first, and I said yes. David stood behind Elias, fury on his face.

I thought it was romantic back then how jealous he was, but last night it vexed me, and I thought of how I cowered, not speaking my mind on little things, wanting to please David. Even when I disagreed deep down.

'Joy, what's wrong?" Violet asked.

"Nothing," I blurted.

"Your eyes look sad," Violet continued. "My *Mamm* had sad eyes sometimes. That's when she'd go pick pink roses. You need pink roses."

I smiled. "Maybe I do."

Daisy, busy making a pink turtle, divulged more information. "*Jah*, *Mamm* would cry when she and *Daed* had a fight. It got loud sometimes. *Mamm* could really yell."

Uncle Micah's brows furrowed. "We all lose our tempers at times."

"Not like *Mamm*. I miss her sometimes but not much. *Daed* is happier, too."

Violet's face turned crimson. "*Jah*, it's quiet now. Is it wrong to not miss your *mamm*? Joy, do you miss your family?"

The girls were obviously honest and would appreciate me being honest, too. "*Nee*, I don't miss anyone back home. I've only been here for a month though."

"Will you stay here?" Violet asked, eyes hopeful. "We'd miss you if you left."

I wanted to scoop up Violet in my arms. "You're so sweet."

Violet beamed. "*Danki*. But you never told me why you're sad."

"Well, I was going to be married, but I might not be now. And that makes me sad."

Daisy whispered something in Violet's ear and they giggled.

Uncle Micah corrected them. "It's not polite to tell secrets in front of someone."

"Do you want us to tell you?" Daisy asked.

Uncle Micah wiggled his bushy eyebrows comically. "Would I want to know?"

They nodded.

"Then tell us your secret."

They held hands and came around the table towards me. "We've been asking God to give my *daed* a wife and us a new *mamm*. And we think it's Joy!" Daisy quipped.

I chuckled at them, trying to appear like adults. "It's that easy, *jah*? Just forget about the man back in Ohio and marry your *daed*?"

Their heads bobbled, and they chanted, "We're going to have a *mamm*. We're going to have a *mamm*."

Uncle Micah's eyes bulged. "Girls, how about you show Aunt Naomi your dough animals."

They ran to get their creations and find Naomi.

Uncle Micah gingerly got up and poured a glass of lemonade. "Want some?"

"*Nee*, I'm fine."

"*Nee*, Joy, you are not. You're losing weight and the sun should have given you a tan, yet you're pale. Are you eating?"

I'd been pushing my food around but not taking many

bites. "No appetite. Must be the heat. And the air's so dry."

His eyes filled with concern. "When Lena came to live with us, she became malnourished, even though she had the best Amish cook in Pennsylvania right here in this kitchen. I don't want that to happen to you."

"*Danki*, Micah. I'll eat lots of salads straight from the garden and watch myself. I suppose I've been so focused on solving my troubles, I'm letting myself go."

Uncle Micah took some pink dough and kneaded it. "Do you want to talk about it?"

I sat across from him. "*Jah*, I do. What would you do if you were me? One day I'm ready to go home and give in, the next I'm determined never to go back."

He steepled his fingers. "I think you should go back home and be Church of the Brethren and marry your fiancé."

I jerked upright. "What?"

"*Jah*, forget about your baptismal vow. It's just a vow."

His face was grave. He was serious. "I'm Amish. How could you suggest such a thing?"

"Because you're so miserable, to the point of not eating."

"Well, God said the narrow road was hard."

"Is that what you're on?"

I nodded vehemently. "*Jah*, I am. I was heartbroken when my *daed* died, but the People were there for me. And when Aunt Abigail died, the same thing. And I see how *Mamm* and others are running from their problems and are on the easy path," I spat out. "Lily wants to leave for modern conveniences. They're all looking for the path of least resistance when my Bible tells me that can be dangerous." I inhaled loudly, not realizing I'd been rattling on without taking a breath.

A smile split his face. "I pushed you to see where you stand, and I think you know now. And I admire you. How did you become such a faithful Amish woman?"

My chin quivered. "It all started when my *daed* got diagnosed with cancer. I had to lean on God. And of course, my *daed* was the most faithful Amish man alive. I must take after him in some small way…"

Micah reached over and squeezed my hand. "I think you do."

Chapter 9

Nathan came over for the noon meal and to see his girls. After a filling meal, he asked me for a private chat in the parlor, away from the guests. When we sat across from each other on the loveseats, the dream of us running through fields of roses made my throat constrict, and I felt so embarrassed. I had to remind myself to stop admiring the shell of this man and see his interior. Looks were like gift wrapping paper and what was inside was the real gift. But, Nathan had such gorgeous wrapping.

"Are you okay, Joy?" he asked.

"*Jah*. Sure. I'm right as rain. *Jah*, I'm dandy fine."

He eyed me suspiciously. "Really? When under such a trial?"

I gulped and nodded awkwardly.

He stared at the flowers on the coffee table. "Uncle Micah and Aunt Naomi are worried about you, and maybe my story can help you." He rotated a shoulder as if to work out a sore spot. "You see, I know you're engaged to a man who wants to leave the Amish. I also know your sister wants you to go back and be in her wedding to an Outsider."

"Really?"

"*Jah*. Uncle Micah told me. It's hard to talk about my wife. Patty and I both lived at the same Amish settlement not far from here. Our parents were like real family, but mine moved to Lancaster when I was in sixth grade. Patty's family bought a big farm here in Punxsy. We wrote for years and sometimes I'd visit. When I was eighteen, Patty's *mamm* asked when I was going to propose. She said Patty never courted anyone because she was staying true to me. Patty assumed we had a commitment. A long story short, I married Patty the next year. I never loved her, but was sure it would come. We were miserable. Her parents blame me for the brain aneurism."

This man's gentle nature shone through, and tears pricked my eyes. "I'm so sorry, Nathan."

"Well," he continued, "I think why I want to share my story is because I acted too hastily, and don't want you to make the same mistake. I felt pressured to marry. It's not right. You shouldn't feel pressured by your fiancé. Aunt

Naomi's been telling you to take walks and find solitude. It's because it helps you calm down and think straight. It also lets you see all that God created and there's something mighty calming about that. We can see by the changing seasons that the autumn leaves don't change overnight, but slowly."

Aunt Naomi entered the room with a plate of pink frosted cookies. "Don't mean to interrupt. *Yinz* can munch on these. The girls made them for you, Nathan."

He thanked her and Aunt Naomi threw me a covert wink. *What on earth?*

Nathan grabbed a cookie and without skipping a beat, continued. "I love to farm because I learn so much about the Lord. He's faithful to make seeds grow, faithful to give us rain or send help. But above all, I feel his pleasure when out in the fields when I'm all alone, with no distractions. I miss my girls, but I know I need this time to seek God about many things." He interlaced his fingers. "Am I making any sense at all?" he asked with a shy smile.

Ach, this is what I needed to hear. "Aunt Naomi told me to spend a week in solitude and I felt this knowing that I should come to Pennsylvania. You're making a lot of sense. But my sister is getting married in a month. Can God show me in a month what to do?"

His eyes were blue pools of tranquility. "Be a part of an Ex-Amish wedding? It's forbidden even to attend..."

He was right, but I couldn't accept it. All our lives, Charity and I talked about our weddings. Our hope chests were full to the brim and many nights we took out dishes, quilts and whatnot, discussing our plans. "Nathan, I know a secret that could stop the wedding and make my family and fiancé wake up to a lot of deceit. Should I tell my bishop back home?"

He jutted his chin and crossed his arms. "Maybe. I'd have to know more details, but one man can't deceive so many people unless they like what he has to say. Maybe the problem is your family wants to leave the Amish and this man convinced them."

I sank back into the couch. "They had no doubts until my Aunt Abigail died in a buggy accident." I looked at him with a sudden revelation. "You're right. Paul can't convince me to leave because I don't want to. My family and the others must have had doubts for a while. Like you said, autumn leaves don't change colors overnight."

Nathan seemed to feel the ache in my heart, such empathy on his face. "If there's any way I can help, let me know. If the girls are too much, I can have someone else watch them."

I sprang forward. "*Nee.* I love them. They make me laugh."

He chuckled. "Me, too. But get some time alone and seek God. Like I said, He's faithful."

My heart lifted. "I will."

~*~

A letter arrived every day over the next week, *Mamm* telling me details of Charity's wedding, but I paid no heed. I took Nathan's advice and spent many a day out in nature alone. Uncle Micah was so kind to keep Daisy and Violet occupied with all things pink. As twilight set in, I had a holy nudge, as Aunt Naomi called it, to not attend Charity's wedding. Such a wise woman. I'd also tell her about Charity's condition. I'd promised her I wouldn't tell a soul, but that was her attempt to hide sin.

One letter from David gave me hope. He was leading up a hay drive and a truck full of hay was expected to arrive this week. And David was coming. The talk we had on the phone must have helped. This was a *wunderbar* gut sign, but I refused to get my hopes up. What I wanted more in life was peace. That awesome peace of God that I found in solitude. I couldn't live a life of seclusion, of course. But I knew worry was the opposite of peace. Trying to figure everything out was the opposite of peace. My fears of the future were the opposite of peace. A scripture that sunk into my heart was, 'Let the peace of God rule in your heart'. I looked up the word *rule* in the Greek Lexicon and it meant 'serve as umpire'. That was easy to understand since I played baseball as a *kinner*. A call needed to be made in a split second, so I suppose I could make decisions right quick too, led by the peace in my heart.

I suppose I'd been doing this for many years. Maybe it was why my resolve to remain Amish couldn't be shaken. My heart was firm on this matter. I had to open my mind to the possibility that my family, even David, did not have this steadfastness.

Was it possible they were following God's will? I'd never say this to other Amish, but recalling my conversation with Sarah coming out in the van from Ohio, she was right. There's been divisions among the Amish and Mennonites for centuries, and most arose from a matter of conscience. Jeremiah said he'd searched all things and he needed to have a clear conscience. It went against my grain to break a vow, but the Bible was clear concerning judging others.

~*~

Today, after Aunt Naomi and I were done washing clothes and pinning them to the clothesline, we put our feet up, and sipped root beer in the Adirondack chairs near the kitchen garden. And I broached the topic of Charity's pregnancy.

"Aunt Naomi, remember about that secret I was keeping?"

"*Jah.* Are you ready to stop carrying it on your own?" she asked with a wink.

My lips felt like lead, but I murmured, "Charity is pregnant. It's why there's a rush for her to get married before anyone finds out. Also, Paul is an atheist and they plan to leave the church altogether after the wedding."

Aunt Naomi leaned forward, coughing to beat the band. She beat her chest and gasped, tears streaming down her face. I darted to her, slapping her back. Was she choking? When she could breathe easy, she exclaimed, "Went down the wrong pipe. *Ach*, Joy, this is horrible. What are you going to do?"

My brows rose. "I was hoping you could tell me."

"I'm too shocked to think. *Ach*, my heavens. I need to

talk to Micah. Get some advice." She twisted up her lips. "*Nee*, we have order in the Amish community. Order that keeps the peace. Joy, you must write and tell your bishop. This is *his* problem. It's too big for you. *Ach*, poor child."

Stunned, I realized how great my pride was. "You're right. I'm already dealing with having an estranged family and maybe losing my fiancé. How could I think of solving this problem that would affect our entire church district?" I took a sip of root beer. "I'll write the bishop tonight, even though I'd be breaking another vow. I vowed not to tell, but what I'm seeing is I'm being asked to cover up sin."

"*Jah*, you are and it's not fair to you. We all know we fall and have struggles, but we help each other out. Joy, maybe the bishop and elders could help. Make the families leaving see reason."

"How could I be so *ferhoodled?* Why didn't I just go to him in the first place? I'm so…"

"Loyal," Aunt Naomi said. "But like any virtue, it can be taken to an extreme. Take meekness for example. Lena is so gentle and meek, but that's what got her into an abusive marriage. Meeting Ruth helped her speak up."

I cleared my throat. "I also decided to not go to the wedding and when David comes, if he's not willing to stay

Amish, I'll let him go."

"When David comes? He's coming here?" Aunt Naomi asked, tension in her voice.

"*Jah*, he's coming in the hay relief truck next week. He set it up. He has experience with these relief efforts."

Aunt Naomi shuddered. "Are you strong enough to see him? Be honest, Joy. Can you truly let him go?"

Peace enveloped me. "Jah, I can."

Aunt Naomi couldn't hide her smile. Her eyes twinkled in delight. "*Gut*. You're Amish."

"Aunt Naomi, I know Andy Weaver's been here to see me along with others, but I'm not fickle. I'm not going to go fall for some Amish man anytime soon."

~*~

Uncle Micah and Nathan threw a pink ball to the twins and they squealed with delight. "*Danki* for the pink ball, Joy," Daisy yelled over to me as I shucked peas given to us from Lancaster Amish. They'd heard of the drought and send truckloads of produce.

"Joy, too tired to throw the ball with us? Need to sit down?" Uncle Micah quipped, mischief in his eyes.

"I need to take care of these peas. Tomorrow we're pickling beets. Why? Are you tired?"

"*Jah.* Tired of yacking to all the men who came to visit you today. I'm going to sell tickets. Only three visitors a day."

I felt heat rush to my cheeks. "Those men came to see you."

He chuckled. "Then why were they asking you if you needed help with this and that? Women's work. And they talk to you when they visit. Joy, you need to pick one of these fine men and forget that unfaithful young buck out in Ohio."

I fumbled and near spilled the peas. "Uncle Micah. How can you say that?"

"Because it's the truth." He threw the ball to Daisy. "Don't you agree, Nathan?"

Now my stomach did a flip. What did Nathan think of me? Why should I care?"

"I think it depends on who came to visit? Who came?" Nathan asked.

"Andy Weaver, but he got bruises again. Staring at Joy out in the garden and stepped on a rake and it sprung up and wacked him."

"*Mamm* always told us it's not nice to stare. When people in town stare at us, I feel like hiding," Daisy said.

"When they take out their cameras, I hide my face."

"That's right, Daisy," Nathan encouraged. "Who else?" he asked.

"*Ach*, Roman Fisher. Now, all the girls have their eye on him, but he went away mighty discouraged. I guess our Joy didn't flirt like the others."

"Of course, I didn't. I'm not a flirt," I said squarely, wondering what Uncle Micah was really up to. Was he trying to make Nathan jealous? Why such nonsense talk?

"And then there was Jacob Miller. Joy, I saw you blush when he came around."

I gawked. "I was canning vegetables! It was over eighty degrees today."

Uncle Micah turned to Nathan. "She's a modest one. It's a *gut* thing men and women sit on opposite sides at *Gmay* because Joy would have herself surrounded by eager whippersnappers."

This was enough. I picked up my peas and headed towards the house when the twins protested. "You said you'd help us catch fireflies. I just saw one turn its light on."

Agitated at Uncle Micah, I pointed to him. "He loves fire flies. Ask him."

"But we want you," Violet begged. "And you promised."

"I'll be right back. Need to get these peas inside and talk to Aunt Naomi about something." I turned and stormed towards the house as the girls clapped their hands in delight, chanting 'fireflies, fireflies!' I never let the screen door slam, but did this time, hoping Uncle Micah heard. I found Aunt Naomi crocheting in her parlor. "What's this all about?"

Her head shot up. "Joy, you scared me. Is everything okay?"

"*Nee*, it is not. Uncle Micah's out there trying to provoke Nathan by saying how many men come calling."

Aunt Naomi motioned to the loveseat opposite her, and I took a seat. "Why are you so emotional?"

"Because I'm embarrassed is why."

"Why do you care what Nathan thinks of you?"

"I don't know," I sputtered. "I feel...embarrassed."

Aunt Naomi set aside the dish towels she was making. "Micah's on a new medicine for his arthritis pain. Mustn't be working. He jokes around to hide his pain."

I felt like such a fool. "Really? He never complains of arthritis pain. Where is it?"

"Mostly in his lower back. He'd be in here with me if he wasn't trying to help the girls so much, but they do cheer him up."

I slumped back. "I feel like an idiot."

"You like Nathan. I can tell. And Joy, it's all right. He's one of the best men I know."

I felt too tired to disagree. "I'm engaged."

"Well, we'll see what happens when David comes. Did you write to your bishop?"

I nodded. "A few days ago. Was so hard. Maybe that's why I'm so emotional. I've been put in such an awkward position. *Mamm* will be furious, as will David. But, like you said, we have our rules and order for a reason."

The phone rang, and Aunt Naomi looked too content to rise. "I'll get it." I ran to the phone and after my greeting I heard David's voice, and he wasn't happy. "David, calm down."

Just then, Nathan came in to get lemonade out of the refrigerator.

"Joy! Joy!"

"I can hear you, David. No need to yell."

"*Jah*, there is. You ratted on us. Told the bishop. How could you, Joy? You promised. You gave your word. That's not acting very Amish."

I wanted to cry, never hearing this tone from David, but tried to steady my voice. "We have an *Ordnung*. We have order. You never should have told me such a secret. It was against our rules and too much to ask."

Nathan sat at the table, fidgeting with his straw hat. *Why didn't he leave?*

"Joy, I thought I knew you, but you have no heart. You wouldn't mind if I lost my land, my dream of farming, just to stay Amish."

I couldn't speak but turned so Nathan wouldn't see the tears welling up.

"Joy, you there?"

"*Jah*, I'm here."

"Your *mamm* wants to know if you'll come back when the relief crew comes out in a few days. She said there's things to get done before Charity's wedding."

"I'm not going," I was able to say, but then the tears spilled over. "David, don't you see how hard this is for me? I can't be in a non-Amish wedding. And I wrote you about Paul. How could you support such a thing! Getting married because they have to."

I felt strong hands on my shoulders. I turned, and

Nathan was standing there, eyes tender. "Want you to know I'm here for you. You're doing the right thing as an Amish person."

"Who is that?" David yelled.

"A friend." My eyes met Nathans. "A very *gut* friend." I dropped the phone and let Nathan embrace me. I *was* fickle. I was starting to care for this man.

"Don't expect me to come out with the relief effort. Call me when you wake up and realize what you're missing, Joy Hershberger."

Silence.

"Joy? Are you there? Joy!"

Nathan reached down and hung up the phone. I felt awkward yet wonderful in his arms. Soon two little girls were jumping, shouting, "We got a new *mamm*! We got a new *mamm*!"

Chapter 10

I was undone the next morning, so Aunt Naomi insisted I go to spinning circle. I'd been avoiding the group, so I wouldn't get attached, assuming I'd be moving back to Sugar Hollow. My only hope literally was the order set forth in the Amish church for discipline. Outsiders thought us harsh having rules, but they were like fences, Aunt Naomi said at breakfast. She'd been to Niagara Falls and said she was thankful for the safety railing or she'd never had stepped up to admire the falls. She said that she felt confident that the lack of rules was making my family feel mighty uncomfortable, afraid and nervous. As for David, his words stung too deeply. It would take time to heal. My mind was so jumpy. Why did I think of Nathan when I thought of David, as if they were intertwined? *Good looks.* They were both such handsome men and I started to think I was shallow.

I followed Aunt Naomi into the circle of friends, five

spinning wheels humming. Ruth appeared mighty uncomfortable, carrying her twins all in front. But, she was the happiest pregnant woman ever. I brought my embroidery, my quilt for the twins nearly done. Lena's beautiful turquoise eyes crinkled as she greeted me. She led me into her kitchen and shook an envelope. "Look what I got in the mail," she said.

I could tell it was a circle letter from the thickness. "Anyone from Ohio in that letter?"

Lena grinned. "No one from Ohio, but talk about Sugar Hollow splitting among the Amish in your *Gmay*. Lena, someone said they heard the families were making peace."

"*Ach*, did they mention which family?"

Lena flipped through many pages and scanned the words. "Here it is. This letter's from Indiana who has friends in Sugar Hollow. She says:

Have you ever heard of such a thing? Three families leaving the Amish and all keeping it a secret. My friend was in a dry goods store and they didn't know she was in there. They talked about a girl out in Punxsutawney who needed to come home before they'd all leave. Can you believe that? It's like a mutiny. (My husband reads about our ancestors coming to America on boats and how some got so sick and tired they wanted to throw the captain over. Not Amish of course.) Well, if that doesn't take the cake. They're having secret meetings, planning to leave, trying to get others to leave, too. But they kept saying that they wouldn't leave until the girl from Punxsutawney came home.

Do you know this girl, Lena? Will she leave the Amish? If you know her, tell her I feel so badly for her. Imagine that girl's whole family leaving and she must shun them? Don't hear that happening every day.

How is the drought? Tell us about it…

Lena folded the letter. "Joy, seems like country gossip about the split is going around the grapevine. I got this letter nearly two weeks ago and didn't feel it was my place to share it, but my aunt said you got a tongue lashing from your fiancé about telling the bishop. I believe he already knew. The Amish grapevine is faster than the internet, *jah*?" She forced a smile. "There's more to the letter, but some of it seems not true? Only gossip?"

"What is it? Maybe I can shed some light on an ugly rumor."

Lena shifted. "Joy, is your sister pregnant?"

"She is," I exclaimed. "People are talking about it? She couldn't be showing yet." As soon as these words flew out,

I knew it must be true. Did Paul pressure everyone because she was further along?

"Sit down, Joy. You're pale. I thought the letter would give you hope that their resolve to leave is weakening, and they won't leave without you. Don't you see? Your family is teetering."

"I hope so. I really love them and we need to be a family again."

Ruth waddled into the kitchen. "Lena, do you have an ice pack?"

"Are you hurt?" Lena asked.

"*Nee*, hot! Need to put in on my neck for a spell."

As Lena got an icepack, Ruth took a seat. "How are you, Joy? You look upset."

"You know all about my family leaving the Amish, *jah*?"

She nodded. "I feel for you. Must be hard. Lena being estranged from her sister is harder on her than she thought. We keep a prayer journal and put your name in." She leaned forward as if ready to tell a secret. "I wrote something in the journal the other day that sounds like a man chewing tobacco would write. Promise not to laugh?"

I nodded, wondering where this conversation was

headed.

"Self-pity is thanklessness. That makes the acronym S.P.I.T. Spit. When I'm feeling that old sinking feeling, I spit. Get it? I remember self-pity is thanklessness and I start to name all I have to be grateful for. I start to rise out of my gloom."

"Spit?" I asked, wrinkling my nose. "Spitting is gross."

"Jesus spit in a blind man's eyes to heal him," Ruth informed. "And in Revelation it says, 'God will spit lukewarm Christians out of his mouth.' What's so gross about spitting? *Bopplin* spit up."

I grinned at this woman's enthusiasm. "Sorry. Never thought of it like that. But, you think it's self-pity that I'm estranged from my family? It's crushing me."

"*Ach*, of course it is. But we're no *gut* to others around us when we're glum. The gloom starts to steal our joy and we know the joy of the Lord is our strength. What if things iron out and you are on *gut* terms in a year or two from now? All the fretting is just a waste of time and energy."

I tried to soak this in. What if things changed all for the better, my parents realizing just how Amish they were, while I stewed out here in Punxsy. Wasted days. "Ruth, you're right."

"Take one day at a time. God gives us daily bread, not enough for a month. We need to go to Him daily to get our strength and it's enough."

I stared at this radiant woman who always encouraged others…until I remembered the twins saying staring was rude.

~*~

When we got home, I saw a stack of letters on the table for me. The one with the bishop's return address, I ripped it open right there and then:

Joy,

Thank you for your letter. I should have reached out to see how you were weeks ago when I found out about the discontent among the People. I thought it was just rumors until I talked to the families who want to leave. I'm not sure, but it appears your family is reconsidering for many reasons, some I think are private family matters.

Be encouraged. Trust in God. And write to me if you need help of any kind.

Bishop Thomas

I hugged the letter. *Ach*, I hope they don't leave the People. But, until I find out, I'm going to S.P.I.T. When I fall into self-pity I'll give thanks for all that's around me here in Punxsutawney. The more I'm here, the more I have to be thankful for.

The girls flew down the steps, dressed in light mauve. Aunt Naomi told them they looked pretty in 'almost pink' dresses, and they giggled. They were wearing mauve, but pink enough for them. I'd be putting these girls on my gratitude list. I needed to see through all the haze around me. Being so absorbed in my problems only made me turn inward, not seeing the blessings all around.

"Will you take us for a walk to the library?" Daisy asked.

Aunt Naomi said it was a lovely afternoon to return the books and replenish their pile. So, off we went, each girl holding a hand. "You girls have learned to read so early. You have a *gut* teacher."

"*Oma* sends us books and corrects our letters," Violet said. Her pink lips frowned. "She lives far away now."

"She's coming to visit us," Daisy informed.

Violet looked up at me. "Joy, why won't you marry *Daed*? If we had a *mamm*, *Grossmammi* wouldn't have to take us to her house."

I stopped. "You're not going to her house. You live with us. I'm watching you, *jah*?"

"*Grossmammi* thinks that us living in a P&P isn't *gut* for us."

"B&B," Violet said. "It means bed and breakfast."

I'd come to love these girls so quickly, as if I'd known them for years. Maybe they were taking the place of my little sisters. We crossed the street and continued to the library. The girls were too quiet. "When's your *grossmammi* coming?" I asked again.

Daisy and Violet stole a glance at each other. "We're not supposed to tell."

I gasped. "Does your *daed* know?"

"*Nee*," Daisy said. "*Grossmammi* sent a letter to her friend and gave it to us. She said to not tell *Daed*. It's a surprise."

This was outrageous. It was obvious that their *grossmammi* wanted to come to confront Nathan and catch him off guard. "Well, it's not right to not tell your *Daed*. No one should tell you to keep a secret from your *daed*."

The girls had gripped my hands tighter and I knew they were nervous. When we entered the library, Helen greeted us. The girls chippered up, amused by Helen's hot pink streaked hair. She told them it wasn't Kool-Aid, but dye that stayed in. They clapped their hands. I told the girls to go pick out books, so I could see them through the glass wall. Soon, they were running towards the children's section.

"Helen, I'm glad to see you. I'm upset."

"What did I do?"

"*Ach*, nothing. I need advice."

She bellowed out a laugh. "Not many people ask me for advice, but shoot."

"The twins' *grossmammi* is coming here from Lancaster and told the girls to keep it a secret. She wants to raise them herself."

"She's a jerk," Helen murmured. "Very controlling woman and her daughter was a chip off the old block. Don't mean to be disrespectful of the dead, but I couldn't stand Nathan's wife. She refused to talk to me because I was a bad influence on her girls. Nathan had to bring the sweetie pie girls to the library."

An ember in me started to burn. A longing to help Nathan. I needed to throw water on any feelings for Nathan, but it was getting very challenging.

"Helen, could you talk to the girls. Verify what they told me and tell Nathan?"

"Me?" she asked, beating her chest. "Why me? Why not tell him yourself?"

"I, ah, don't want to get involved in something so personal."

Helen blinked rapidly and covered her mouth. "You're blushing!" She raised fingers as she counted. "Eight. Now there's *eight* Amish women in love with Nathan."

I cupped my cheeks. "I'm not blushing! It's a hot day."

"So, you just start to blush in air conditioning? Fess up. Hey, if I was Amish, I'd be chasing Nathan myself."

I took up a flier and fanned my face. "I'm engaged to someone out in Ohio."

"Whatever," Helen said as she stooped down to gather books and headed to the fiction section to shelve them.

I followed. "Helen, will you talk to Nathan? He's your friend and – "

"Safe? Not Amish? If you get more emotionally involved in his life you'd have to break things off with your fiancé?"

I was dumbfounded at Helen's frankness. Rudeness. "Okay, I'll tell him. We're just friends."

Helen let out a laugh that made everyone in the library look up from their books. "If you say so."

Chapter 11

The girls were bushed by seven o'clock and so was I, so after finishing chores, I headed to bed. I kept waking up, worrying about Nathan. He needed to be informed that his mother-in-law was writing to his girls in a way that was less than forthright.

The wind whipped up, and stones hit the window. Hail? *Ach, nee!* What little crops were growing couldn't be ruined by hail? I ran to shut the window, fearing a thunderstorm was coming in, but the hail stopped abruptly.

"Joy!" someone yelled from outside.

"*Jah*? Uncle Micah? Is everything okay?"

"It's David. Meet me on the front porch."

He ran off before I could give a reply. Was I dreaming? What was he doing here? I slipped on my robe, wrapped my hair, and secured my prayer *kapp*. Tip toeing down the steps, I paused. The last time I talked to David he was furious. He must have had a change of heart.

When I looked at the clock at the bottom of the steps it read four o'clock. It wasn't the middle of the night, as I rose at five most days.

I saw movement by the front door and opened it to greet David.

He drew me into his arms. "Joy, I've missed you."

Why did I feel nothing? I backed away. "What are you doing here?"

"I came with the hay drive. Remember? It's this week. We brought a semi full of round hay bales."

I sat on a rocker, avoiding the loveseat. "You said you weren't coming. Remember our talk on the phone?" I stiffened. "You said I had no heart, didn't care if you lost your land, just to stay Amish. Have you changed your mind? Will you return to the People?"

David knelt before me. "Joy, I'm still confused. My *mamm* is weakening since she found out about Charity's pregnancy. That threw us all. The ministers have talked to my parents and they just need time to think. We need you back home because you're so…Amish. Joy, how can you have no doubts?"

I looked at him with pity. He was so double-minded. David was easily swayed to leave the Amish over land. He was greedy.

"You don't need me," I said evenly. "You need to listen to the church elders and the bishop. I have a job here and have come to feel at home."

David gripped my shoulders. "I heard a man's voice when we talked. "You're in love with someone else. Who is he?"

"David, you're hurting my arms!" I pulled away and stood on shaky knees.

"Who is he!" David yelled.

The door opened and Daisy, eyes wide, put her fists on her hips. "She's going to marry my *daed*.! Joy, you won't leave us, will you?"

I took Daisy's hand. "*Nee*, honey."

"Who are these kids?" David growled, exasperated.

"I'm Daisy Good and my sister is Violet Good. *Daed's* Nathan Good and he's going to marry Joy!"

Aunt Naomi stepped out on the porch. "David, what are you doing here? And I heard yelling. Come in for coffee and let's talk."

As the dawn chased away the dark, David's spiteful scowl was clearly seen. He didn't even look like the David I knew. Had he tasted the forbidden fruit and changed so quickly?

"Naomi, did you ask Joy to come out here to marry this little girls *daed*?"

Aunt Naomi gasped, and then her belly started to jiggle. "Boy, your imagination's run wild."

"*Nee*," Daisy corrected. "*Daed* said he's going to marry Joy someday." She smiled, revealing a missing front tooth. "Joy, I told *Daed* all about *Grossmammi* coming and he said don't worry because Joy will be taking care of you, not *Grossmammi*. And you have to get married if you're going to live at our farm." She covered her mouth as if now realizing she said too much. "I wasn't supposed to tell you. *Daed* likes you a lot."

"Okay, Daisy," Aunt Naomi ordered, "back to the table for breakfast."

David glared at me. He didn't look hurt, but just mad. It was like he lost a bid at the auction. If he loved me, he'd show signs of sorrow, but *nee*, he was losing control and didn't like it.

"David, I'm not marrying anybody for a while. Don't consider me as your fiancé until you've won my heart back, because you've changed. I don't feel like I know you."

He collapsed onto the loveseat. "I don't know what I

believe anymore. Joy, I need you."

I sat next to him. "Take time to figure it out. Remember when I took that week off to just rest and be quiet? The dust will settle and the real David will emerge. Will you do that?"

He gripped my hands. "Will you come back to Sugar Hollow? You can go back with us. Lots of room in the van."

I bit my lower lip. "Bishop Thomas wrote and said my family has private matters he didn't want to put in a letter. Does he know about Charity being pregnant?"

David gazed at me with pity. "It's hard not to know. She's showing. Joy, you need to come back and find these things out for yourself."

I gripped my stomach as pain shot threw it. "I need time to think. I won't come back with you, but there are vans headed out to Sugar Hollow all the time. Or I could ride the bus. I'd want Aunt Naomi to be with me, so we'd have to make arrangements."

"Why does she have to come?" David asked with a scoff.

"She's not afraid to speak up. She saw through Paul before any of us did. And, well, she's become like a real aunt to me. It's like she filled in the hole Aunt Abigail left."

David gripped my arm again. "You love someone else. I can see it when you look at me."

I didn't deny it but restated that I needed time to think. David backed away, cowering like a wounded animal. Part of me wanted to sooth him, another part of me wanted to tell him to grow up.

~*~

David stopped by later in the day, chipper, as if nothing irked him. We enjoyed a good meal along with other guests at the B&B, including the twins. David asked if we could talk in the parlor afterwards and so we situated ourselves on a loveseat. He took my hand. "I was a grump this morning. Sorry about that."

"It was early..."

Our private talk was short lived when tall, lanky Andy Weaver entered the room. "Stopped by to see how you were, Joy." He plumped down in the other loveseat and turned to David. "*Danki* for the hay drive. With so much help coming in from the People, it makes me grateful I'm Amish. What do people do on their own?"

David cleared his throat and shot me a glare. "Well, people go to churches that help just as much."

Andy scratched his clean-shaven chin. "Not like the Amish."

"Like the Amish, minus the rules," David said curtly.

Soon I heard Benjamin's voice, the sweet short yet stalky Amish friend who'd stopped by to play checkers with Uncle Micah. "Hi Joy. Came over to play a game. You look busy, though."

I motioned for him to come in and take a seat. "The four of us can play Scrabble."

"Sounds fun to me."

David narrowed his eyes. "I'm going back to Ohio and have something important to discuss with my fiancé. Can we have some privacy?"

The two men stood, giving me puzzled looks, and left the room. David's jaw was rigid. "Joy, how can you encourage other men when we're engaged?"

How could things deteriorate between David and me so quickly. "I don't encourage them. They just come. Sometimes to visit Aunt Naomi and Uncle Micah."

"I don't like it, so please stop."

Astonished, I sprung up and ran from the room. Aunt Naomi was hard at work washing dishes and I needed to help. Of course David followed, demanding that we resume our talk.

"I'm helping Aunt Naomi with the dishes. David, I told you to go back home, pray, and wait for answers. I have nothing else to say."

"I do. Charity is expecting a call from you. She's over at my house to use my *mamm's* cellphone."

"Cellphone? Lily has a cellphone?"

He nodded, making no excuse for her, but pulling a cellphone from his pocket. "You can use mine. *Mamm* told me it's really important."

The room started to sway, or was I? David had a cellphone?

"You can use the B&B landline," Aunt Naomi said. "You can hear better."

I gave David a suspicious look. "You're sure this is important?"

"Charity called me today and said it was. It's why I stopped by. She didn't tell me the details, but just wants to talk to you."

There was too much noise in the kitchen, voices from the living room spilling in. "David, dial your phone and get Charity on the line, but I want to talk to her from my bedroom."

"Fine," he said, tapping a few buttons until the phone rang. David asked his *mamm* to put Charity on the phone and I grabbed it, running up the stairs. "Charity, is that you?"

"*Jah*. So *gut* to hear your voice. I'm walking outside so…" There was a pause and then she continued. "Joy, I need you here with me. I had a miscarriage yesterday and now Paul has called off the wedding."

She let out a heart-wrenching wail, and I could only try to console her. Paul was so despicable. He never loved Charity, only used her. My sister struggled to talk. "Joy, we're not leaving the Amish. You were right. We were all bitter. *Mamm* is getting counseling for grief and taking some medicine. But David's family is leaving for sure. As your stupid, silly sister, learn from my mistake. Don't go after David because you love him. Love that's not the right kind made me lose my senses." Another gasp and more sobs.

My family wasn't leaving the Amish. Praise be! As much as I felt for Charity, I wanted to shout for joy. My dear family. No matter where I lived, I could go home to an Amish family. Intuitively, I saw myself staying in Pennsylvania for a while.

"Will you come home?"

"I, ah, am watching twins and helping Aunt Naomi. Charity, it's so nice out here. Not many tourists and…how are people treating you since they found out you were pregnant?"

A long groan. "No one says anything, but I feel judged. I repented, you know. I made a confession to the People last Sunday."

"You should move here," I blurted. "There's all kinds of jobs and…let me talk to Aunt Naomi."

"Joy, I can't. *Mamm's* not too *gut*. I need to help take care of the *kinner*."

"How about for a vacation? Maybe the whole family could come. I miss you all so much."

A long pause. "I'll ask *Mamm*, but she sleeps a lot. Joy, she's very depressed."

This was indeed sobering news. "Like last winter when we thought she had the flu?"

"*Jah*. At least she's not hiding her depression now. I'm low, too. I felt that *boppli* kick, you know."

What was I to do? Go home with David? I needed to take care of my family. I needed to talk to Aunt Naomi.

Chapter 12

After the twins were tucked into bed, and I was assured that they were asleep, not able to overhear, I sat with Aunt Naomi on the front porch. She seemed deep in thought, head down. "Is everything okay?"

"*Ach, jah.* Long day. Sit down a spell." She slid to one end of the porch swing, making room for me. "It's so hot tonight. Eighty degrees after nine o'clock. So unusual."

As we swayed, it cooled me a bit. "Any rain in the forecast?"

"*Nee.* Fields are turning brown, did you notice? Water may need to be hauled in." She sighed with a din. "Got more cancellations, too. Who wants to see Pennsylvania's green rolling hills when they're brown?"

Aunt Naomi was a rock, and this melancholy was out of character for her. I'd put off getting advice until tomorrow, when she was rested.

"What's on your mind?"

"*Ach,* nothing," I lied. "Just came outside to sit."

Aunt Naomi slipped me a wry smile. "Spill the beans. That David of yours upset you, *jah?*"

"Well, a little bit. It's Charity. She had a miscarriage, and Paul's broken things off." My face burnt hot. "I asked her to come out here for a vacation, but she won't leave my *mamm.* She's going through another depression and hardly gets out of bed."

Making the swing come to a halt, she eyed me. "You're going back to Ohio, aren't you?"

I wasn't expecting Aunt Naomi to be so attached to me; her voice was full of feeling. "That's what I want to talk to you about. My sister feels disgraced. She's repented and my family is going to remain faithful to the People."

"Praise be," Aunt Naomi quipped. "And David's family?"

"*Nee.* And I'm breaking things off with him for *gut.* Charity said she lost her head over Paul, compromised her morals and faith. She warned me never to change for a man."

"That's right," Aunt Naomi said. "Micah loves me for who I am. Nothing better on earth than to be truly loved, with your faults and all." She took my hand. "I'm sorry,

Joy, but I don't see that in David. I see it in Andy Weaver, though. But maybe a bit too much. He'd be like an obedient pup to you, not a real man. *Nee*, Andy needs someone who can follow him. Now, Nathan, he's my favorite of all your admirers."

I withdrew my hand. "You're imagining things. Nathan and I are…"

"Getting attached in a short time. I see it and he admits it, Joy."

I gulped. "He said that?"

"*Jah*, overheard him talking to Micah."

Now my face was on fire, as well as my heart. "Are you sure you heard right?"

She nodded. "*Jah*, for sure."

"I've only known Nathan for a short time. I was supposed to marry David in November. I haven't even called things off yet. I just don't see things as clearly as I used to."

"Since you met Nathan?" she prodded, a tease in her tone.

I couldn't admit it out loud. It was outlandish. "I'm not so fickle."

"Joy, I know two brides who kept their wedding date,

but switched the grooms. *Ach*, the stories I hear from guests. An Amish woman thinks of marriage all her life, her hope chest started when she's twelve or so, *jah*? So when they start to unpack that chest, what they imagined all those years ago leaves them wanting."

"Wanting a new fiancé?" I sputtered. "That's ridiculous."

Aunt Naomi started to giggle. "It's true, though. Their eyes were open and Mr. Right came walking by." She squeezed my hand. "Is this you, Joy?"

"How? How can you…read me? Well, maybe David's weird behavior was obvious to us both. He's tied to his *mamm's* apron strings and I don't find it appealing when I think of marriage. But, I didn't come out here to talk to you about marriage. I'll be an old *maidel* and accept it. My question is can you spare me? Could you and Uncle Micah watch the twins if I leave for a while?"

Aunt Naomi's eyes grew round as buttons. "Heavens no. But, don't you worry. There's plenty of single women who'd take care of those girls in a heartbeat."

"But I'll be back…"

"You never thought you'd stay this long in Punxsy, did you? When you get back to Ohio and your family, you'll feel settled there. Just remember to write me."

I flung my arms around this dear woman. "I don't want to leave. I never knew I'd feel so at home in Pennsylvania."

"You can visit," Aunt Naomi said, her voice cracking. "And you can call me on the phone, *jah*?"

I knew I had to go, but Aunt Naomi was wrong. I'd come back. Pennsylvania suited me right fine.

~*~

I packed hastily that night, but it didn't take long, as I only brought one suitcase. I had a fitful night sleep, sorrow flooding me. Saying good-bye to the twins would be agony, especially when they believed I'd be their *mamm*.

David showed up for breakfast and asked if I'd made up my mind to go back to Ohio. When I told him I would, he wrapped his arms around me, exclaiming 'that's my girl'. I shivered. His touch was not welcome, nor the condescending way he assumed he owned me.

After breakfast, Daisy tugged at my apron, asking why I was sad. The time had come. I must look at these two girls I loved, yes loved, and tell them I was going away. I knelt and scooped them into my arms. "I'm so glad you girls can read and write, because we'll need to talk that way for a while."

Violet put her palms up. "Why, when we can just talk?"

"My *mamm* is sick and I need to help her. But, I'll be back in a jiffy."

"How long's a jiffy?" Daisy asked, chin quivering.

"Two weeks?"

"That's too long," Violet sulked. "Take us with you."

I blinked. "I don't know if your *daed* will say yes to that. And I have my *mamm* to care for."

"Did she go to the doctor?" Daisy asked, eyes filling with tears. "Sick people go to doctors and take medicine. Did she get her medicine?"

"You have a twin sister," Violet stated gruffly. "Why can't she do it?"

How could I tell them my sister needed me for her sick heart? "Well, we have a store to run, and it's too much work."

Violet broke into a sob and squeezed my neck. "But, you're going to be our *mamm*."

I wish! I wanted to holler. "I'll send you something pink every day. Would you like that?"

"Every day?" Daisy asked, a drop of cheer in her

voice.

"Every day. We have a store full of things and I can ship them out."

Violet released me. "I'd like a little quilt only with pink string, not red like the one you finished."

"I'll make you one, then. That quilt is for my twin sisters. It's another reason for me to go home. I made that for their birthday present. They love kittens and they can hang it on their bedroom wall."

David started to hurry me, saying the van pulled up, but to my shock, Nathan ran into the kitchen. "It's raining! Praise God! It's raining!"

Uncle Micah charged outside and we all followed him. He did a little jig and threw his arms in the air. "*Danki*, God! Much needed rain!" He twirled Aunt Naomi around and hugged her. "A nice gentle soaker, like I was praying for."

The twins grabbed Nathan's hands and they ran around in a circle. They asked me to join them, and I did. Nathan joined the twin's hands together and he took mine and we embraced. It was all so natural. Nathan held my head to his chest. "Joy, I'm so relieved."

I heard his heart thump and then a deafening crack

exploded and then blinding lightning. I heard Aunt Naomi yell for everyone to get inside, and Nathan and I ran hand in hand. When I saw David standing there, hands deep in his pockets, scowling at Nathan, I stopped short. I didn't let go of Nathan's hand. It was all too wonderful.

Nathan whispered in my ear he had something important to ask me. I nodded, even though the pain in David's eyes sank me low. I never wanted to hurt David. When we got into the parlor, Nathan locked the door, and gazed at me, eyes full of... *love.* "Joy, I can't help it. I love you. I know we've only known each other for a few months, but it's real. Will you marry me?"

To my utter shock, I sat down and cried. Tears of joy! A man like Nathan wanted to marry me? "I'd break too many hearts," I said, an attempt at a joke.

He sat beside me, taking my hand. "*Nee*, that's what I'd do. You have as many men trying to get your attention as Aunt Naomi has clothes pins."

I laughed. What a peculiar analogy. "I string them along, *jah*?" I asked, more humor to distract from my shock and shyness. Nathan looked like he wanted to kiss me, and I was so afraid. I'd lose my heart for sure.

But as we stared at each other, neither of us knowing

what to say, we bowed in for the sweetest kiss.

"Can I take that as a yes?" he asked.

"I need to go back to Ohio!" I blurted. "What am I thinking." I shot up, pacing the floor. "You don't know, but my *mamm's* in bad shape. My sister, too. I got a call last night near begging me to go out and help."

Nathan shrugged. "That's not an answer. We can write and can take our time. Love is patient, *jah*?"

This man disarmed me. David wasn't this kind, but rather demanding. Memories of meeting at the kissing bridge shamed me. Nathan had a steadiness about him that anchored me. I wanted to say yes. "Nathan, I've tried to hide how I care for you, but I need time to get to know you and my own mind. My mind's been in a jumble about my family and the split among the People."

"I understand. Don't answer me now if you don't have an answer you can keep. We'll write and maybe I can bring the twins out for a visit."

I ran to him and boldly sat on his lap. "I'd love to say yes, but I need time."

He kissed my cheek. "You've broken your engagement to David, *jah*? He's leaving the Amish?"

I leaned my head on his chest. "*Jah*, for sure. Even if

he was to stay Amish, I've seen his behavior up against yours. David didn't bring out the best in me."

He kissed the top of my prayer *kapp*. "We'll miss you so much. I wonder who I can get to watch my girls?"

My eyes bugged. "Not Sarah or Tabitha Miller!"

He chuckled. "I'll send you a list and you can pick."

"Are you serious?"

"*Nee*. You need to trust me. It's the most important part of marriage."

Marriage. The word left a *wunderbar gut* taste in my mouth.

~*~

"The rain across Western Pennsylvania was a tease. Less than a quarter inch of rain fell, lasting an hour. And no clouds on the horizon." I heard KDKA Pittsburgh Radio sound throughout the van. "Oh, no!" I exclaimed, but no one could relate. They were all heading back home to lush Ohio.

I pulled out stationery from my tote and began to write, but David leaned near me. "Who you writing to?"

An alarm went off in my mind. No, a confirmation. David was too controlling and the sooner I broke things off the better. But in a van?

"You writing to that Nathan?" he scowled.

"I'm writing to him and the twins. And then I'll write to Aunt Naomi and then to Lena, Ruth, Ivy, Rose and Serena if you must know. All my friends back in Pennsylvania." I paused to collect myself. "David, I don't think you realize how serious this drought is. The water table is so low, wells could go dry. I wish I could have taken the twins back to Ohio with me."

He groaned. "You care too much about those twins and not enough about your sisters."

"*Ach*, David," I glowered. "Such harsh words. I made them a quilt for their birthday to hang on the wall." I slammed down my pad of paper on my lap. "Why do I have to defend myself to you?" I was glad there was lots of chatter in the van so no one could hear. "You don't love me, David. It's over between us, and I can't be won back."

I turned away, staring at level green fields. Cows were out to pasture, ducks glided in ponds. A lush land I had no desire to return to.

"You're just upset, Joy. Come on. I'll stay Amish for you if you want." He caught my chin so I'd look at him. "I'll forgive you for falling for that Nathan. You were in a Grand Canyon valley of trials and he was your friend.

When you see your family and Sugar Hollow, you'll be your old self."

"David, stop it. You don't understand me at all. I'm not the same person anymore. And I see more clearly things I was blinded to."

"Such as?" he challenged.

"David, you still see me as a little girl with braids and I still see you as the mischievous boy at school that made me laugh. We've known each other our whole lives." I wiped a sweaty palm against my apron. "You either don't accept or won't see that I'm a grown woman."

He was quiet for a spell. Was he actually listening?

"And I don't want anyone to be Amish for me. I want a man who is Amish and loves it, like my *daed* did. I don't see that in you at all."

More silence. David was being too quiet. I glanced his way to see his expression, but he had none. He was giving me the cold shoulder. From my talks with Rose at spinning circle, there were many ways to control people and silence was one. He was discarding my words as useless. Well, if that's what he was going to do, I'd write letters.

By the time the van pulled into Sugar Hollow, I'd written everyone on my list. David darted out the door after it stopped in front of my family's store. Charity was there, arms open, with a smile that blew the misery of the past three hours in that van, being snubbed by David, out the window.

Chapter 13

"*Ach*, Joy, so glad you're home," Charity exclaimed as we embraced.

I wanted to cry, my dear sister was so pale and thin. "I've missed you."

We locked hands and passed by a group of older Amish women who greeted me but stared bleakly at Charity. I remembered the twins saying it's not polite to stare, but didn't dare speak so rude to my elders. Charity's cheeks were beet red and I realized quickly the trial she had endured. We entered the store, Charity flipped the sign to closed, and we unfolded wooden chairs and sat behind the counter. "David looked upset. Want to talk?"

I nodded. "I broke things off. He's not Amish." I fumbled for words lurking deep within about Nathan, but I was too concerned for Charity. And I didn't want to upset her that I planned to return to Pennsylvania.

"Well, that's *gut*. David's changed. But, Joy, does it hurt so much? You and David were inseparable."

I slipped stray hair under my prayer *kapp*. "It was *gut* for me to be in Pennsylvania. Punxsutawney isn't a busy tourist place." I hesitated to ask, but Charity looked forlorn. "The miscarriage and the wedding being called off. Does it hurt so much?"

Charity's chin quivered. "*Jah*, it does. I still care for him, despite all his faults. He was different when alone. But it was you who turned our whole family back to reason. We were all looking for greener pastures, that utopia you talked about." She let out a long sigh. "I never knew how hard shame is to carry."

I wrapped my arms around my sister, rubbed her back and sang the *Loblied*. Charity joined in half way. Tears trickled down both our faces. We'd never expected so much change and pain since spring.

Charity's cry became animal-like, as she howled. What a cruel taskmaster sin was. She was forgiven, but sin was leaving scars. I knew my sister. She said no one would marry her. She was an old *maidel* before being old. The image of Andy Weaver ran through my mind. I'd had too stressful a ride home and needed some rest.

~*~

That night I cooked up all of *Mamm's* favorite foods: roast beef, mashed potatoes, green beans and brownies for dessert. I ran out to the kitchen garden to make a big salad and it shocked me at how lush it was compared to Aunt Naomi's.

The twins ran out with buckets, telling me *mamm* wanted some tomatoes picked to make her energy drink. May and Marge were two little cuties like Violet and Daisy, only they were not towheads, but brunettes, like me. My heart sank. I missed the girls already, but they'd get my letter soon.

"Joy, do you think we're taller?" May asked. "Esther Weaver said we are."

"She did? Well, you're growing, but not like weeds. I'd say you're just right."

They plunked tomatoes in their tin buckets. May broke into a laugh. "Esther came here a lot when you were gone. I think she's going to marry Shiloh." She cupped her toothless grin and giggled.

"Shiloh get married? He's only nineteen." I dismissed the notion until Shiloh came whistling up from the barn.

"I'll marry Esther for her cookin'," he said, tongue in

cheek.

I laughed. "The way to a man's heart, but you're not a man."

He snapped his suspenders and flexed his arm muscles. "I am, too. And maybe I will marry Esther. Maybe we're secretly engaged."

Shiloh was a tease, so I just motioned for him to go away, but when Esther showed up for dinner, I was a bit put out. I wanted to catch up with my family, and she wasn't a sister. But as we all chattered, Esther had a lot of input and seemed like she fit right in. I studied Shiloh's face. His tender expression towards Esther told me he may not be kidding. Was he engaged? And how did my little *bruder* grow up so much in my absence of two months? Sadly, I realized Shiloh didn't need me anymore.

Everyone was kind and there was no lack in conversation, but as I dried the dishes, loneliness cast a net over me. I was homesick…for Pennsylvania. For Nathan and the girls.

"What's on your mind, Joy?" *Mamm* asked, trying to be chipper.

"Did Esther come here a lot when I was gone?"

"She was here to fill in many gaps. Joy, you know

I'm battling depression, getting grief counseling and all. Esther was here on many low days for me. Her steadfast Amish ways reminded me of you. And we all got to thinking how deceived we were. The *Gmay* has been so kind and helpful, but Esther sat up with me at night, talking on the front porch. She's had pain in her life, you know, living with her aunt and uncle when her parents passed."

I thought of Aunt Naomi and how blessed she was to raise Lena and so many others who called her 'aunt'. "Well, I'm sure they appreciate having Esther, since there's six boys in that family."

Mamm scrubbed a stubborn stain in her pot. "I'm starting to see we have losses and gains, and that God has a plan. It's a comfort to know He has a plan. Esther says that all the time."

I couldn't help but ask. "Does Esther have a plan for Shiloh?"

Mamm's face split open with a smile. "I hope so. It would be nice to have one of my *kinner* married. Charity told me you and David have called things off."

"I broke things off. He's not Amish…"

"And?" *Mamm* prodded.

159

"And I'll only marry an Amish man."

"David hasn't made up his mind yet. Talked to Lily and they may remain Amish." She cleared her throat. "You got a letter from Pennsylvania. Nathan Good. Who's he?"

I stopped drying the dish. "Nathan? He sent me a letter already?"

Mamm wiped sweat from her brow. "Did you meet someone in Pennsylvania?"

I could feel that I was blushing, so I fanned myself. "Getting so hot in here. Nathan's a friend. Met lots of people in Punxsy. I had so many come calling, I was surprised. There's a man who I think would fit Charity."

Mamm instantly took a chair and slowly closed her eyes. "Your sister will never marry."

My brows shot up. "She's asked for forgiveness."

Mamm swooshed at the air. "Sure. They all forgive, but Joy, no Amish man will marry her. Talk of Charity's pregnancy is known for miles around and many witnessed it here when she was showing."

My mind was racing. Racing to Andy Weaver again. "*Mamm*, her past could be left here if she goes to live in Punxsy."

Mamm bit a knuckle and tears sprang from her eyes. "Joy, you just got back. I want my kinner near. Too much change for me, and this darkness that comes."

I bent down and hugged my dear *mamm*. She tried to hide her depression but failed. She needed me here for a while. Nathan said he'd wait, but how long? And why was Nathan always on my mind?

~*~

When the night was still and everyone was in bed, I stole away with an oil lamp to the porch. I wanted to savor every ounce of Nathan's letter. I opened it to read:

Dear Joy,

I miss you already. Maybe it's because you're always on my mind. The twins talk about you all day and at night they ask if we can pray for you. The girls miss living at the B&B, too. Maddie Fisher is coming here during the day and Helen stops in quite a bit.

I paused to thank God it was Maddie who would be looking after the twins. A lonely widow, not one of the many girls trying to capture Nathan's heart.

The rain we got left as fast as it came in. Many folk's wells are going dry but we can buy water by the truckload to fill our tanks. It's not cheap. The hay drives have helped. My cattle are fed for now. What people fear is a heavy downpour and flash flooding.

We trust God.

Now, enough about boring day to day stuff. Joy, I miss you not because of the girls. I can't get over how fast I got attached to you. Maybe it was because I thought you weren't available and someone safe to talk to. I planned to stay a bachelor because my marriage was a nightmare. But, Joy, I know God created marriage and everything he makes is good. I've been seeking him and I feel this great love I have for you is an answer to prayer. On lonely days I'd pray that I'd find someone to love. When I did, I was afraid I'd kill her, like some say I killed Patty. Well, I had lots of time during this drought to seek His face. I also took books out of the library to understand brain aneurisms. They have nothing to do with stress. You might think me stupid for thinking I killed Patty, but my inability to love her ate at her heart and well, I thought I made her blood pressure go up.

Joy, I didn't have to try to love you. It took me by surprise, but it came naturally. As naturally as the autumn leaves turn colors.

How is your mamm doing? Is there a history of depression in your family? I read about that in the library, too. It can be hereditary. I'd ask around.

How's your sister. I pray for your whole family, but especially for you.

I love you,

Nathan

Once again, I was humbled that a man like Nathan could love me. I held the letter to my heart, knowing I'd accept his proposal, but how? My *mamm* needed me. I scanned the letter again. *Depression could be hereditary?* Tomorrow I'd go talk to my *grossmammi* and ask her questions about her breakdown after Aunt Abigail's death. But, she was so tightlipped. Would she tell me anything?

~*~

After chores, I ran barefoot to the little *dawdyhaus* on the farthest corner of our two acres. How they loved the woods and nature. *Grossdaddi* attracted over seventy types of birds. *Grossmammi* reveled in her flower garden and upon seeing all the pink flowers, I thought how much Daisy and Violet would enjoy them.

My *grossdadd* waved as he poured sunflower seeds into feeders on the porch. "*Gut* to see you, Joy. Missed you something awful."

I ran to him and kissed his cheek. "Missed you, too. But it seems like things got sorted out here when I was gone. No one in the family turning English?"

He groaned. "*Nee*, no one in our clan, but that David

of you're is still trying."

"What? He said he'd turn Amish for me."

Grossdaddi took a seat on the porch swing and motioned for me to come sit. "Joy, marriage is a weighty thing. You need to have no doubts and turn over every stone. People can hide things."

He seemed to be talking about himself, regret in his voice. "Is that what you did?"

His face grew ridged. "*Ach*, we all have our faults."

That was not an answer. "Is *Grossmammi* home?"

"She's at a canning bee. Making lots of jam from all the berries the women picked." He put an arm around me. "Something's troubling you."

I leaned into him. " *Jah*, I have questions about my *mamm's* depression. Someone told me it can be hereditary and I remember *Grossmammi's* breakdown after Aunt Abigail's death. I hate bringing it up, but my *mamm* doesn't want me to go back to Pennsylvania...and I want to."

He squeezed my shoulder. "Meet someone out there?"

I gasped and blinked. "How do you know?"

He chuckled. "You've got a skip in your step, and I

know it's not David who put it there."

"Promise you won't tell anyone?" I asked evenly.

"Well, can't promise you that if it's an Englisher."

"He's Amish and we became fast friends and it led to romance. We're writing. He's asked me to marry him."

He grabbed my knee and shook it playfully. "*Gut* for you. And I can tell you love him. But, you're torn between making your *mamm* happy and this fellow."

"Nathan Good's his name."

"Nathan Good. You'll be Joy Good when married. It fits you. Well, will you accept? Or maybe you already have?"

"I want to be sure. Turn over every rock, like you said. But I can't see Nathan if *Mamm* wants me to stay here in Ohio. So, can you shed any light on depression and if it runs in the family?"

He let out a mournful whistle. "Well, when your *grossmammi* had her breakdown we'd just lost Abigail. It was normal to have such grief. But your *grossmammi* went to the hospital and it was pitiful. She hugged a doll, calling her Abigail. She'd stare at a blank wall for hours. The doctors said she had a lack of a chemical in her brain. He asked her lots of questions when she was up to it, after she came back to us, and she admitted to having a darkness come over her out of nowhere. No rhyme or reason. They said she had moderate clinical depression, and so does your *mamm*." He put up a hand. "Now, this is between you and me. Abigail never showed any signs of depression, chipper as a song bird. She reminds me of you." His eyes filled with tears as he yanked his handkerchief from his pocket and dabbed his eyes. "The death of a child, you never get over."

My poor *grossdaddi*. He was opening up, telling this family secret hidden too long. "Aunt Abigail was one of my favorite people. So caring towards everyone."

"*Ach*, she cared too much." *Grossdaddi's* voice quaked. "Never should have gone out on that buggy ride to help Mary Graber. Lost her life helping someone whose dog died? Mary should have come to Abigail's, not her go out in all that rain." He shook my knee again. "It's not your job to make others happy, Joy. We all have our cross to bear. Your *mamm* will be fine. So many from the *Gmay* have been over. She's not alone. And she's been through trials before, like your *daed's* death. She'll cry and all if you leave, but you need to live your life."

I was confused. "But aren't we supposed to take care

of our parents?"

He pulled at his gray beard. "In their old age!"

He tried to lighten the conversation, calling out the names of the birds in his feeders, but my mind was elsewhere. But in his animated way, he turned to me, eyes wide. "Your *mamm* was raised on a farm. Never saw her unhappy. God made a garden to put humans in, not stores. Your *mamm* would do better on a farm, but land prices are too high."

"Not in Punxsy!" I jumped up and clasped my hands, plans forming in my mind. "So many Amish and Mennonites are buying up land in Western Pennsylvania."

He stood and embraced me. "You're so much like Abigail. Always the optimist. But, I don't see your *mamm* moving to Pennsylvania."

I hugged him tight. "I think there's a man out there for Charity. She'd have a new life away from all her shame."

"Well, if that's the case, take her out for a visit. Esther Weaver and Shiloh can hold down the shop. They're always together."

I rest my head on his chest. "I love you *Grossdaddi.*"

"And I you, child. And I you."

Chapter 14

The next day, after weeding our vegetable garden and bringing in an abundance of produce, I headed over to the store. It looked crisp with the new coat of white paint Shiloh slathered on yesterday.

As I turned the sign to *open*, a buggy pulled up. The work day had commenced. But this was not a customer. It was David, and he extended a bunch of wildflowers to me. "*Danki*," I said. "Do you need to buy something?"

He came back around the counter, like when we were courting, and gathered me in his arms. "I can't lose you, Joy. I'll do anything."

His grip was too tight. "David, let go. Customers might come in."

"Can I pick you up for lunch? I'll pack a picnic."

I wanted to remain friends with David, but not court him. "You're always welcome to share a family meal with us. Charity's making chicken and dumplings today. Stop by at noon."

He jutted his chin in defiance. "I want time alone with you."

As he wouldn't move, I stepped around him and went to the canned goods that needed unloaded. As I stacked cans, he gripped my arm. "Joy, I can't lose you. Do you understand? I love you. What can I do to make things right?"

His voice was pressured and he scared me. Hopefully Jeremiah would appear soon. "David, things change."

He twisted my wrist as he yanked me towards him. "You've changed. It's that new guy out in Punxsutawney. I saw how you ran with him when it rained. I'm not blind."

I yelped as the pain in my arm shot up to my shoulder. "Let go!"

"Confess. You've been unfaithful to me."

Was I dreaming? If so, this was a nightmare. "David, my arm!"

"Admit you love that Nathan guy!" David screamed in my face.

I'd never seen such fierceness in him. "David, calm down."

"*Nee*, admit it. You're in love with someone else!"

Anger started as a small stirring and then it erupted like a volcano. "*Jah*, I am. Nathan would never treat me like this."

David's wild eyes raged, as if a rabid animal. He shoved me up against the shelves in disgust, but I lost my footing and tripped over a box and thumped my head on the wooden floor. David continued to spew out all manner of hateful things, but all I could feel was the pain in body and soul.

"What's going on here?" Jeremiah cried out. "Joy, are you okay?"

"She tripped over a box. I was just about to help her out."

Jeremiah put his face within inches of David's and told him to leave the store and never come back. David exploded on Jeremiah, but he ran to the back door and called for Shiloh. David was no match for Shiloh. Being pacifists, Shiloh wouldn't fight, but along with Jeremiah they could grab him and escort him out.

Why I felt so humiliated, I didn't know. But shame shot through me, as if I did something wrong. Had I?

After David left, Jeremiah picked me up and held me close. He told Shiloh to grab a blanket for sale and wrap it around his sister. I was shivering, being in shock."

~*~

Charity hovered over me, giving me fresh ice packs. The bruise on my face throbbed. "Charity, I can't go out in public like this. What will I say happened? I tripped over a box?"

Charity's eyes were ablaze with fire. "You tell them David pushed you. Joy, we both fell for such awful men."

"I can't ruin David's reputation. And people wouldn't believe me."

Charity and I held hands as we swung on the porch swing, but my face and arm hurt too much and I slipped over to the glider. "Charity, I think David is more spirited because his *daed* isn't."

Charity sighed. "Jonas? He's a jellyfish. Lily's the outspoken one in that marriage, for sure."

"David's embarrassed of him, you know. Says he's afraid of his own shadow, so David had to learn from others how to be a man. I think Lily doesn't respect him either."

Charity narrowed her eyes. "They never did look like a happy couple. You don't think…"

"What?"

"It's just a thought, but Lily could divorce Jonas if she left the Amish. Something is at the root of their decision to leave, and Lily's the one insisting."

It was very strange. Jonas was a dedicated Amish man. People thought he had no backbone but followed Lily like a newborn pup, but he was devout. "How can we find out?"

Charity sipped her lemonade. "Do we have to? I don't have much emotional energy these days."

"You're right. Jeremiah can handle it. He saw David screaming over me. I'd never seen him so furious." I readjusted the icepack. "He's a *gut daed*. He makes *mamm* so happy, despite her bout with depression, she feels nurtured, don't you think?"

Charity nodded. "Wish I could meet someone like Jeremiah." She rose. "Well, I best get back to the kitchen. *Mamm's* having a hard day and that leaves the canning up to me and Esther."

"Esther? Is she here?"

"She will be," Charity said. "I love that girl. She's perfect for Shiloh and helps *mamm* cheer up."

We heard the familiar whistle of our *grossdaddi* as he rounded the corner. "How are my favorite *grosskinner*?" He ran up the porch steps as spry as a teenager but stopped abruptly when seeing me. "Honey, you get hurt?"

Charity spoke up. "David pushed her into a shelf and she fell."

Fire and wrath darted from *Grossdaddi's* eyes. "Just like his *grossdaddi*. I'm having words."

"*Nee*," I begged. "Let things calm down."

He shook a long finger. "No one hurts my Joy without getting an earful from me." He spun around and ran down the steps over towards the horse barn.

Charity cheered him on. What on earth? Why did he want to have words with David's *grossdaddi* but not his *daed*?

~*~

I yearned to go back to Pennsylvania, but I couldn't run from my problems, my disappointments, my pain, my shock. David's cruel behavior haunted me. I moped around the house, staying away from the store. My cheek was swollen and red and my arm ached. I was so grateful it was an off Sunday tomorrow so I wouldn't have to see anyone. Hide my face. Hide my shame.

A tap on my bedroom door, and *Mamm* slipped in. "Can we talk?"

"*Jah, Mamm*."

She settled herself in my rocker. "The Mast family has agreed to come to a reconciliation dinner with the bishop." *Mamm* leaned her head back on the rocker and began to sway. "How are you, Joy? I never knew you and David could fight like you did."

My heart raced and a pain shot through my stomach. I held back tears for *Mamm's* sake. Too many tears in this house, I reasoned. "I had time to think of David while in Pennsylvania. David was nice to me always, but we never disagreed. When I refused to leave the Amish, David became too pushy and when he came out with the hay relief, many said he acted arrogant. I'm glad it all happened. Might have married the wrong man."

Mamm shifted in the chair. "But if we have a reconciliation dinner…"

Mamm wasn't seeing things clearly. She saw the adorable David as usual. She wanted me to marry someone local, it was clear. She wanted all her *kinner* close-by in Sugar Hollow. "So, when's the reconciliation dinner?"

Mamm gave me a knowing smile. "Tuesday. A slow day at the store. Charity told me you both think Lily wants a divorce, and that's her reason for leaving." She hugged herself. "Jeremiah's been my comfort this past year. I was

175

twice blessed in love. If Lily is that unhappy, deep down I feel sorry for her."

Such tender words. "You said you'd never marry after *Daed* died. What made you marry Jeremiah?"

Her smile broadened. "He was patient with me. I was like a turtle coming out of its shell, real timid. But he waited. And he accepts me with all my thorns and faults."

"*Ach, Mamm*, you're a *gut* woman and real pretty," I said.

"Not when Jeremiah was pursuing me. I didn't want to marry again and told him real plain-like. He asked if he could just be my friend. I hardly knew him, yet somehow when we talked, it seemed like I always had. The Lord put us together, I suppose."

Did I dare tell *Mamm* about Nathan? This is exactly how I felt about him. Like we'd always known each other.

"I believe everything will come out in the dinner. David will confess, and you will forgive. He's been so stressed about his *mamm* wanting to leave the Amish, and thinking he lost you to another man. He snapped, and I know what that's like. My nerves make me say unkind things, as you know."

I didn't have the heart to tell *Mamm* I wouldn't be

marrying David. Not only did I doubt his character, but my heart was at home in Pennsylvania.

Mamm pulled a few letters from her apron pocket. "Got this letter and forgot to give it to you. From that Nathan out in Pennsylvania. He upsets me, Joy. He'll take you away from us."

What *Grossdaddi* said about *Mamm* being raised on the farm around nature came to mind. "*Mamm*, do you know you can buy a farm in Punxsy for dirt cheap. *Grossdaddi* thinks living on a farm would be *gut* for your nerves. You liked it out there so much when we visited two years back."

She arched her neck. "We have the store here."

"And with all the responsibilities, maybe it's a strain on you. We were made to be outside in nature. It calms my soul. Took long walks in Pennsylvania to hear that still small voice of God."

Mamm leaned forward. "When I was a *kinner*, I'd sit in the hayloft and watch the stars. God felt so close. It was a slower paced life."

"And wouldn't you like that again? Land prices are dear here, but many Amish and Mennonites are leaving Lancaster and Holmes County to find land in Western Pennsylvania. They have some of the cheapest land prices in the nation."

Mamm again rest her head on the rocker. "Jeremiah loves his store." She closed her eyes and rocked. "Sounds lovely though."

Mamm was so tired. Too tired. Her eyelids were half pulled down shades. *Lord, lead us.*

~*~

When Mamm left, I ripped open my letter.

Dear Joy,

This will be a quick note. It's not that I don't miss you, but there was a fire last night and I'm worn out. My English neighbors down the road had a bonfire and they thought they'd soaked ground all around it. They didn't know the undergrowth was dry and it took off. I was up all night helping.

The girls miss you and so do I. My in-laws are coming for a visit which has me nervous. I don't mind them visiting my girls, but they always get around to talking about raising them, since they think I'll never remarry. Can I tell them I have hopes to remarry?

Joy, I don't want to pressure you. If we write for a year, I'll be fine. I want what's best for you. How is your mamm coming along? And Charity? Is she still feeling disgraced? I think Andy Weaver would stumble and break his nose if she came out. You're identical right? If so, he'd stare at Charity and not look where he's going.

Miss you more than I can express. Maybe the twins and I will come out to visit after this drought is over. For now, we're keeping an eye on our fields. Many Amish youth in Rumspringa smoke and it concerns me.

The flowers were pressed by the twins.

Love you,

Nathan.

I opened wide the envelope to see tiny pressed pink flowers. The pull to Pennsylvania was oh so strong. Maybe they'd visit? Unbidden tears ran down my cheeks. I was homesick. I needed to hear a voice from back home. I decided right there and then that I needed to talk to Aunt Naomi. I'd go back to the phone shanty and tell her about all that happened with David and ask for prayer for the reconciliation dinner.

~*~

Tuesday morning, I woke up with a knot in my stomach. It didn't go away as the day went on. I felt so alone. Outnumbered. David was the man everyone loved, and I'd be pressured to forgive. Forgiving is one thing, marrying is another. And my heart was turning so unexpectedly. I thought Nathan would vanish when I got home, but he was on my heart always.

Around noon, I started to cry. How could I go through with this meeting? And why did I have to participate? Who did I have to reconcile with? *Mamm* hugged me and told me all would go well, but I was not convinced. At Charity's insistence, I laid down on the porch glider and closed my eyes. But I was soon interrupted by the UPS man who handed me a package. It was addressed to me, so I opened it. Two books tumbled out. *Sarah Plain and Tall* and *Skylark*. A little typed note was on the receipt.

Joy,

I read these books to Daisy and Violet and they said you were their Sarah. How cute. They wanted me to get them for you, so I did. Enjoy. Helen. PS. My hair is purple. The girls have a new favorite color already!

Happiness filled me. I looked at the back of the books to make sense of the note. I soon discovered that Sarah married a widower who had two children. A mail order bride story. And the second book was about how Sarah hated the prairie because of the drought and yearned for Maine with plenty of water.

I hugged the books. The girls were afraid I wouldn't be happy living in Pennsylvania because of the drought?

Oh, their precious young minds. I scanned Helen's note again. *'They said you were their Sarah.'*

I love them! I love him! It was all so plain. I believe the Lord was knitting our hearts together in love, a scripture often quoted at spinning circle. New courage rose up.

Chapter 15

At the reconciliation dinner, David and his parents sat across from *Mamm*, Jeremiah and myself. I'd never seen Lily look so nervous. Bishop Thomas sat in Jeremiah's normal seat at the head of the table.

We ate cold chicken, German potato salad and fried zucchini, a simple meal that Charity whipped up. After the bishop threw down his napkin in approval of the meal, he pulled at a few knuckles and started the conversation. "David, what do you have to say to Joy for your rough treatment?"

David's eyes misted, and he pulled me in with a one-word apology. "Sorry."

"Sorry for what?" Jeremiah snapped, most out of character.

David brows knit. "I'm sorry I lost my temper. I want Joy back, but she keeps pushing me away. I tried to get her attention."

"Attention?" Bishop Thomas grunted. "That's no way to get someone's attention."

David slipped a glance to his *daed*. "I wanted to show her I loved her. That I was a real man, in charge."

"By twisting a woman's arm and shoving her up against a shelf?" Jeremiah bellowed.

Jonas put a hand on Lily's. "We've seen a change in our son. All the dissention has made him unstable. We need stability that only the Amish can provide."

Everyone gasped at Jonas' boldness. Everyone was quiet for a spell, until David got that same raging countenance. "Well, I'm leaving. I won't be a spineless man like you, *Daed. Mamm's* had to depend on me for everything. Major decisions a husband would make."

Lily slid next to her husband. "You don't know much about your *daed*. We talk behind closed doors"

Jonas gripped his wife's hand. "David's right. For too long I've let my timidity make me passive." He faced David. "I don't want you to lose respect for my *daed*, he tried his best, but he was too domineering. I tried to be the opposite. I'm sorry that so much has been put on you."

My heart went out to Jonas. He was very timid. Many times David said his *daed* held the family back financially, lacking motivation. Lily toiled away making quilts that they depended on for a living.

Mamm spoke up. "David, I can relate to your *daed*. Sometimes life can cave our souls in." She slipped a hand through Jeremiah's arm. "This man's kind words have lifted me up out of many a pit. Losing my first husband and then sister has made me a depressed woman. I understand you. Life can wear us down."

Lily wiped a tear and cleared her throat. "I agree. I did learn so much from the Brethren and I thought Jonas could find healing like I did." She turned to David. "*Jah*, for the past year, I've found great comfort in my Bible and urged your *daed* to read it. He can't put it down."

Bishop Thomas clamped a hand on Jonas's shoulder. "I see the change."

Mamm patted my back. "Joy here always said we'd come to our senses in time."

"Well, maybe I'll stay Amish and maybe I won't," David spouted. "I'm willing to try to be more stable and content, but I need Joy's help. She always kept me steady."

Everyone grew quiet. David's eyes landed on me, but I turned away. I felt so indifferent to David. And this had been a very slow change. Like the color of leaves in autumn, they change slowly without me noticing.

"Can I leave?" I asked Bishop Thomas, feeling that I'd done my part. The bishop asked if I forgave David and I said yes. He nodded in agreement and I went up to my room. I was sure David would pressure me again, and I wanted to start the books sent by two little sweethearts who wanted me to be their *mamm*.

Later that day, after finishing *Sarah Plain and Tall*, a loud banging on our front door jolted me out of bed and look out the window. A fire? An accident? I soon heard our English neighbor say she had an urgent message on her cellphone for me. I ran down the stairs and thanked Mrs. Johnson and took the call. "Hello?"

"Joy, this is Aunt Naomi. *Ach*, Joy, there's been a fire. Nathan. He asked for you."

I panicked. "Is Nathan okay?"

"Joy, you must come out."

My knees went weak. "Is Nathan okay?" I repeated.

"The drought. *Ach*, it's Terrible. A fire. Nathan's

asking for you."

I began to tremble. I looked at my *mamm* and then Mrs. Johnson. "How can I get to Pennsylvania?"

"I can go online to check bus schedules," Mrs. Johnson said.

"Aunt Naomi, I'll do all I can to get out there."

"We sent a driver out already to pick you up. Be ready at nine o'clock. Will you come?"

"Of course. Give Nathan my love."

I thought the driver would never appear, but he did. *Mamm* was nervous with me going so far with a male driver, she insisted Charity come with me. I was all too glad to have her by my side.

Mamm hugged me tight. "You go ahead, Joy."

Mamm was being strong for me. "Esther will be here to help you, *jah*? I love you *Mamm*. Tell everyone good-bye. I'll write."

~*~

We got into the B&B at one in the morning, but I was wide awake. "Can you take me to Nathan's farm?" I asked the driver.

"I'm a regular driver for the Amish. They said to bring you here."

I had to wake Charity up and she could barely keep her eyes open. I tried to calm myself by watching the fireflies flicker. It wasn't working. I led Charity to the parlor couch where she resumed her deep sleep. I ran toward the voices coming from the kitchen. Uncle Micah sat surrounded by suety faced English and Amish firefighters "Where's Nathan?"

All heads went down except Uncle Micah. "Joy, come sit down."

My heart leapt into my throat. "He's alive, *jah*? I know there was a fire."

"He's alive," said a burly English firefighter. He reached over the table to shake my hand, but then withdrew. "I'm filthy. My name's Philip West. I'm the fire chief. Nathan's in a burn center in Pittsburgh."

"Can I see him?" I asked. "I can pay for a van. He's asking for me."

Uncle Micah told the men to take the donuts out on the porch and get some fresh air. Their job wasn't over yet. The men cleared out, but one man put an arm on my shoulder. "*Gut* to see you, Joy."

I didn't recognize him; his face was so dark. But then his eyes twinkled. "Andy Weaver?"

"*Jah*, it's me. Such a mess. But, we saved Nathan's house." He walked away with the other men, fatigue pushing his shoulders down.

Uncle Micah told me to sit next to him.

"Why couldn't the driver take me to Nathan? Pittsburgh isn't that far."

Aunt Naomi soon appeared and seeing her tear streaked face made me dizzy.

"Can someone give me some answers?" I asked.

She put on her tea kettle and asked Micah to explain what happened.

"Well," he started, "Nathan's neighbors never did listen to the bonfire warnings. A fire took off and Nathan helped. When it spread to his barn, Daisy ran outside, screaming that she had to get her kittens." He stopped and wiped his brow. "When Nathan saw her run in, he did what any other *daed* would do. He went in after her. *Ach*, the fire was so bad. Violet would have gone in too if Maddie hadn't held her back."

Uncle Micah hung his head as if out of steam to go on.

"You say Nathan is in Pittsburgh?" I prodded.

"*Jah*. Daisy and Nathan. Being treated for smoke

inhalation and burns. I don't know the extent of it."

I felt nauseated. No, this could not be happening. "Nathan asked for me."

"He did. Before he and Violet left on the helicopter to be at the burn center. He kept saying 'Joy' and everyone thought he was trying to be strong. The joy of the Lord is our strength, *jah*? And we know our ancestors were tried by fire and sang to their deaths. But I knew what he meant. He was crying out for you."

But maybe he was trying to encourage Violet. The *kinner* knew this common verse, 'The joy of the Lord is our strength'. They sang a song to memorize that verse. Either way, I never realized how much I loved not only Nathan but the twins. "Can I go to Pittsburgh tomorrow? Take Violet for a visit?"

Aunt Naomi lowered her face, gazing at me like I was *ferhoodled*. "She's too young to visit a burn center. *Nee*, she's upstairs sleeping in your old room. She said it smells like you. That poor child. She needs a *mamm*."

I want to be that woman! I ran upstairs with a determination to serve this dear family in any way possible. I crawled into bed next to Violet. It all seemed so right. That this girl would be my daughter. I was here to comfort her.

~*~

When the rooster crowed the next morning at dawn, I awoke with a start. I slept in? And then it all came rushing back. Violet was still asleep and Nathan and Daisy were in Pittsburgh. The grandparents would be here today.

Lord, help the grandparents feel assured that Daisy and Violet are well taken care of and help me know my place. Help me see what I can do. Ach, Lord, this is a difficult situation. Give me wisdom to know when to speak and when to keep quiet.

When I crawled out of bed, Violet didn't even stir, but whiffled a little snore. I quickly got ready for the day and went downstairs. The couple at the B&B were not familiar. Aunt Naomi was busy making pancakes and I fell into the routine. When I met her at the sink, she introduced me to Mike and Theresa Beiler. They only nodded and asked where Violet was. I informed them she was still asleep.

Mike grimaced. "Too late for Amish *kinner* to get up. And a B&B is no place for my *grosskinner* to be raised."

Aunt Naomi turned when she flipped a pancake and it landed on the counter. Were her nerves as raw as mine?

She turned so the Beilers couldn't see her anger.

I grabbed a cup of coffee and sat across from the Beilers. "Violet is fine for now. I'm glad Maddie held her back from running into the barn after Nathan. Maddie's a *wunderbar gut* woman."

Teresa's eyes brimmed to overflowing with tears. "The twins are so much like their *mamm*. Patty had spirit. Her girls do, too. To think Daisy ran in the barn to save her kittens. That's Patty for sure."

These poor grandparents. They'd lost their daughter and saw her in the girls. Did Nathan see this? Maybe another tragedy triggered fresh grief over their daughter. "Would you like for me to wake Violet up? I'm sure she'll be happy to see you."

Mike swooshed away my idea. "Let her sleep. We're waiting for a driver to get here to take us to see Daisy. She's the one who needs our attention."

Teresa protested, but Mike put a firm hand on hers. That they only mentioned seeing Daisy and not Nathan seemed peculiar. "When is the driver coming?" I asked.

"Fifteen minutes," Teresa said.

Aunt Naomi turned to give me that knowing look. "Mia Stewart is driving. She has room."

Mike eyed me with contempt. "Room for who? From what I understood, only family can visit."

Naomi bowed her head for an uncomfortably long time. I knew she was asking the Lord above for the right words. "I know Patty was a dear girl," she began, "but Nathan is lonely, *jah*? He asked to see Joy."

Teresa held her chest. "*Ach*. What are you saying?"

They looked to me for that answer. "Nathan and I are courting," I said confidently, not any doubt to the outcome.

"Is there a wedding coming up?" Mike barked. "Those *kinner* are coming with us to Lancaster if not."

Stunned, I nodded. "*Jah*, there will be a wedding."

Aunt Naomi's eyes grew too large for her face. She fumbled for words and then changed the subject to Lena and her wedding in the parlor. Mike and Teresa stared as if she was speaking a foreign language. Naomi went on to say some Amish weddings could be whipped together and small, especially if it was a second marriage, which wasn't even true. But in Lena's case it was. *Ach*, poor Naomi. She was too dumbfounded to make sense.

Mike shot me a stern look. "Are you the girl from Ohio?"

"*Jah.* I came back here as soon as I got word."

Mike rolled his eyes. "Aren't you engaged to someone out there? The girls send us letters that some girl named Helen writes for them. Nathan doesn't have the time, I suppose. They said you went back to Ohio to marry someone else."

"Mike," Teresa chided. "The girls also want to paint their house teal." She offered me a warm smile. "Did you hear pink is not their favorite color anymore?"

"Where you engaged not long ago?" Mike blurted.

"There were three families that were going to leave the Amish out in Sugar Hollow. My boyfriend's family was one of them. It was our first big disagreement and some ugly behavior came out of him. I broke things off."

I was relieved to see my sister enter the kitchen. "This is my twin sister, Charity." I took her hand and pulled her to sit next to me. I didn't let go of her hand. "Our family's remaining Amish. I'm not sure about the other two. My best friend, Becky, hasn't written or spoken to me, but I'm praying she remains faithful to her vow."

Charity slipped close to me. "I'm proud in a *gut* way of my sister here. Her firm stand to remain Amish turned our whole family around. You know how it says a rudder of a ship can turn the course of the journey? Well, Joy did that for us." She wrapped an arm around me and kissed my cheek.

Mike looked at me with sudden approval and asked if I was going with them today to see Daisy…and Nathan.

~*~

I sat next to Teresa in the van. She kept staring at me, hesitated, and then looked again. Did I have this morning's breakfast on my face? "What is it, Teresa?"

"I'm sorry. I shouldn't stare. It's not polite."

I tried to lighten the atmosphere. "So Daisy and Violet say."

"I just wondered if you fell or something. You have a bruise on your cheek."

I'd forgotten. I covered it. "I fell."

"*Ach*. That must have been quite a fall."

I remembered Lena saying how she made up excuses for her first husband's abuse. "I fell after my former boyfriend pushed me so hard after twisting my arm." I rubbed my forearm. "It still smarts, but it was worth it to wake me up. I was blinded by David. Like I said, it took a big disagreement for his lower nature to come out.

195

Looking back, he always wanted his way."

"I'm sorry," Teresa said. "Nathan was like that with Patty. It's hard to forgive. Mike is all thorns around Nathan."

I'd prayed this morning for wisdom and I hoped what I had to say was helpful. "Nathan blames himself for Patty's death. But, he got books out of the library and learned there are many causes for aneurisms. I did some reading, too. Some women are born with a blood vessel defect and giving birth to twins can also cause so much stress on a woman's body."

Teresa looked out the window for a spell. "I've read things, too. But, Nathan didn't make Patty happy, and I'm sure it added to the cause of her death."

I took Teresa's hand. "My *daed* died of cancer several years ago. My *mamm* blamed herself for a while. And then her sister died in a buggy accident and she blamed the Amish ban on cars. It was why she wanted to leave." I squeezed Teresa's hand. "We don't know the reason for many things, but we can't judge."

"Judge?" Teresa asked. "I don't judge. We Amish don't judge." She withdrew her hand.

"You're still judging Nathan. I'm sorry. You're older

and wiser, but I see how Nathan is with the twins. He's a great *daed*."

Teresa set her jaw, as if not wanting to hear another word, but a scripture kept rolling around in my mind. "Who are we to judge another man's servant?"

Teresa glared at me. "What?"

That's somewhere in the Bible. We don't have all the facts to judge another person's heart."

Teresa's stone face cracked, her chin began to tremble. "Patty wasn't an easy child to raise. She cried over everything and never outgrew it." She cupped her mouth as if just discovering something. "Mike thought Nathan would change this. Make her happy."

A lump, too big to swallow, filled my throat. I could only hug Teresa, unable to speak. Nathan was their 'cure' for Patty. My love for Nathan grew deeper with each new revelation of this man.

~*~

The grandparents wanted to see Daisy first, and Teresa clung to me, so nervous. Before entering Daisy's hospital room, we heard a man's voice soothing a whimpering child. "I'm sorry. We'll have to ask the nurse."

"Must be the doctor," I mumbled. "Don't want to intrude."

"I do," Mike said, stepping around me to enter the room.

Well, he was Daisy's *grossdaddi* and had the right, I reasoned. Teresa stayed with me, wanting her husband to break it to her gently about Daisy's injuries. But we waited patiently as possible, bracing ourselves, watching wheelchairs with bandaged limbs and some with black masks on, burns apparently on their faces. Daisy's fresh, innocent face flashed before me and I hoped she was unscathed.

We couldn't hear what was being said in the room, but the tone was grim. Teresa said she could stand it no more and went in and I followed her. We could only stare. Daisy was in the hospital bed, her arm wrapped in a bandage and it wasn't the doctor who was with her, but another burn victim. He was trying to encourage Daisy to not be afraid of getting her bandage changed. This man was hooked to an IV pole with liquid bags attached.

"*Jah*, Darling, listen to your *daed*," Mike said.

I clasped a nearby chair. Nathan? He turned to look at Mike but spotted us. Although his voice was husky and a bandage covered one eye, his lips curved into a smile when seeing me. "Joy!" He tried to compose himself, but he was soon shaking with sobs. "I'm so…so glad."

I nudged my way to him, not daring to hug him as my heart longed to do. "Are you badly hurt?"

He raised his right bandaged arm. "This side got the worst of it."

Daisy cried out. "*Ach, Daed*, I'm sorry."

Nathan choked out that she was worth it all. Daisy shocked us all by asking what happened to me. Did I get a burn, too? Why was my face burnt? I told her I tripped and fell. After Nathan calmed down, I went to the other side of the bed. "Daisy, how are you?"

She pointed to her chest. "They keep checking to see if I can breathe." And then her eyes brimmed with tears. "I got a burn on my leg. That fire got me, too. It hurts when they change the bandage. I kept screaming and *Daed* hopped over."

"Hopped?" I asked, turning to Nathan.

"Like I said, the fire got my right side." He tried to grin. "This IV pole doubles as a crutch."

The doctor entered the room, clearing his throat to let his presence known. "Can I take a look at your leg now that your father is here?" He motioned for us to leave, but Nathan's bandaged arm reached out for me. "She can stay."

"Is she the child's mother?" the doctor asked.

"Stepmother to be," I said, my eyes lingering on Nathan's face.

The doctor went on and on about patient privacy rights, that we weren't married yet, but we didn't hear every detail. Nathan leaned to kiss my cheek, but my lips met his. I felt too bold, but pure love shone from Nathan's devoted blue eyes.

Chapter 16

I stayed for a week, Nathan signing papers giving me power of attorney. And he told the doctor we were engaged; Amish didn't wear wedding rings is all. Despite the pain all around me, I had joy deep within. I had not a flicker of a doubt that I was meant to be Nathan's wife. I yearned to talk to Jeremiah, asking him if this is how he felt about marrying my *mamm*. He always treated us all the same, never a burden, but a bonus of sorts.

My mind often wandered to Teresa and Mike *Beiler*. They approved of me? Gave us their blessing? It was clearly difficult for Mike to do, and I doubted his sincerity, but Teresa took me aside. She'd shared with her husband that they'd handpicked Nathan to fix Patty, and it was wrong. Knowing Nathan saved Daisy's life was also to his credit.

So, I had much to ponder, but after seven days,

wounds seemed to miraculously heal enough for them to be released. The doctor said skin grows back naturally, but I saw the divine in it. Bandages would have to be changed at home and home care instructions were given. Nathan's voice gained strength as did his lungs. He wanted me to be in the room to see his face bandages changed, saying if I was repulsed, he wouldn't hold me to a marriage proposal. I couldn't stomach the smell of the burnt flesh, truth be told, so I always found a way out. I was busy with Daisy or making a phone call to the B&B to give them a report.

But not today. Nathan insisted. I sat there, holding his left hand, strong and muscular. He winced as the bandage was removed and asked me to look at him. At this point the nurse left, and I saw the extent of the damage. His eye drooped a little, there was some scarring, but once again, our lips found each other and we offered each other a kiss that was sacred. "I'd love you even if it were worse," I assured him.

We stared at each other until I broke into a laugh. "The twins say it's not polite to stare."

Nathan smirked. "Wait until they're in love." He pulled me closer to steal another kiss and I was at home.

It was as if I really believed this was planned before the foundations of the earth that we were meant to be husband and wife.

~*~

The day that Nathan and Daisy were to come home, a van pulled up right before breakfast, and assuming it was them, I ran out to meet it. When the door opened, out popped *Mamm*, Jeremiah, Shiloh, Esther, May and Marge. "What are you doing here?" I asked while exchanging hugs.

Jeremiah put an arm around me. "We're looking at some land. Joy, I think the papers lie. Land can't be that cheap."

Mamm was radiant. "And Joy, we heard about Nathan and the twins. Wanted to see if we could help in any way." She looked around. "Where's Charity?"

I stifled a giggle. "She's getting ice cream with Andy Weaver. Remember the man I told you about?"

Mamm gasped. "Really? Do you think?"

I offered a knowing nod. "They took Violet to The Country Store to get ice cream and all kinds of goodies to cheer her up." I pulled *Mamm* close. "Why is Esther here? She's not family."

Mamm wiggled her eyebrows. Having never seen this gesture, I was confused. Was *Mamm* annoyed? Happy? She whispered in my ear. "Engaged. Shiloh wants to farm, too. Your *Grossdaddi's* love of farming is in his bones."

I hugged *Mamm*. "And yours. Isn't it lovely out here? And to think we finally got a real soaker. Green should be popping up again soon."

Mamm quickly let me in on some news that she thought I'd find unpleasant. "Joy, it's not so happy out in Ohio. David and Becky. Well, they found something in common. Discontent. And it's spreading."

"David and Becky? *Mamm*, what do you mean by that?"

"*Ach*, she chased him so hard when you left she caught him. And they deserve each other."

I had to admit, this hurt. Becky had been my best friend since we were in diapers. She'd always shown an interest in David, but chased him when she knew we could have been working things out?

"*Ach*, Joy, I'm sorry. I should have waited until later to tell you."

"*Nee*, *Mamm*. Anytime wouldn't be *gut*. I don't care

for David like I used to, but finding a loyal friend is hard to find. I thought Becky was that. And very Amish. I always imagined her being in my wedding."

Jeremiah overheard. "You'll find someone better. Someone who deserves you."

I slipped an arm through his. "We have something in common."

"And what's that?" he asked, a smile splitting his handsome face.

"You married a widow and I'm marrying a widower."

Jeremiah looked over at *Mamm*, confusion etched onto his face. *Mamm* slipped an arm through mine and we were a trio. "I'm engaged to Nathan and I couldn't be happier."

Mamm started to cry and Esther was right by her side. "What is it?"

"You're marrying Shiloh and our Joy is engaged."

"And Charity is seeing someone out here," I added.

Jeremiah lifted his arms in surrender. "Looks like we better look for a big parcel of land so we can build houses next to each other."

I laughed. That would be too *gut* to be true.

~*~

After a hardy breakfast, Aunt Naomi asked Uncle Micah to show Jeremiah and Shiloh the five farms for sale. She called up a van driver as some of the farms were in Smicksburg, ten miles away, and some in Plumville and further south.

When they left, she rubbed her hands together. "Now, we can make wedding plans!" She looked to my *mamm* for approval. "Mary, do you want the wedding here or out in Ohio?"

Mamm pursed her lips. "Esther and Shiloh will wed this November out in our neck of the woods. We could have a double wedding. Joy, what do you think? Esther, do you mind sharing your special day?"

Esther said she didn't mind, but my expression must have given me away.

"You want to wed here?" *Mamm* asked, a trace of hurt in her tone.

I inhaled deeply. Violet came and sat next to me, fidgeting to beat the band. "I'll want my new *dochders* to help prepare, you know. It might be easier here."

Violet hugged me, and then she whispered in my ear, "Where's *Daed* and Daisy?"

Everyone overheard. Aunt Naomi spoke up. "I'm

sorry. I'm so thrilled Nathan and Joy saw the light, I'm stepping into something that's not my business."

"Saw the light?" *Mamm* asked. "You encouraged this relationship?"

Aunt Naomi's merry eyes held mischief. "Joy, do you remember when Nathan talked to you about not being too impulsive? In a roundabout way, we kind of suggested he share his story?"

"*Jah.*"

"And all those pink parties, gardens, and on and on?"

I nodded, looking down at Violet.

Naomi let out a roar. "And how the girls lived here at the B&B? Nathan coming over every day for the noon meal?"

I bat my lashes in disbelief. "You planned it all?"

"Well, the girls started the pink parties, but Micah kept the ball rolling, giving them ideas. Sending you over to tell Nathan this and that. *Ach*, it was clear to us the first time we saw you together you were made for each other. It was that nudging I was trying to tell you about. The *Gut* Lord gave Micah and me this 'knowing' of sorts that you were the one for Nathan. So we prayed and it all fell into place…with a little bit of help from us."

My mind skipped through the summer events. Some were a bit hazy but I soon saw a pattern of Nathan showing up at odd times. After some eligible bachelors came to visit, Nathan came over that night. I started to chuckle. "Aunt Naomi! You pushed us together. *Dankl!*"

Mamm fidgeted a bit. "And did you discourage David when he came out?"

Aunt Naomi rolled her eyes. "No need for that. He was a sour grape. Very disrespectful and too overbearing towards Joy. Micah and I saw her wilt like a dried-up flower, but around Nathan, she bloomed."

Violet raised her arms and clapped. "My *Daed* is a *gut* farmer. He makes things grow." She suddenly started to brood, her lower lip protruding. "He's coming home today, *jah?*"

"He is honey," I assured. "Sometimes getting all the paperwork done to get out of the hospital takes time. Even if they don't arrive until tomorrow, we'll be patient."

Violet leaned into me, trying to hide her disappointment and fears.

Charity near skipped into the kitchen, Andy Weaver

on her heels. She stopped abruptly and Andy bumped into her, catching her before she fell. She took Andy's hand. "*Mamm*, Esther, this is Andy Weaver. We've become fast friends."

I never realized how handsome Andy really was until now. *Mamm* seemed uncomfortable. Afraid. Did she think her *dochder* was immoral enough to fall into sin again? Didn't she realize Paul had enticed her? I asked Charity if she could help me pick greens from the kitchen garden and she bobbed a yes. Violet was my shadow, but I told her I wanted her to really know my *mamm*. She'll be your new *grossmammi*, I reminded her.

When outside, I saw how much this dry garden had grown. "So thankful for the rain. I thought the herbs were dead, but the water brought them back to life." I picked some basil. "It's like a miracle."

Charity asked what to pick, but I asked her if we could chat. We sat in the Adirondack chairs and my sister seemed to create an instant wall. "I know what you're thinking," she said, cheeks red.

"Sister, you're wrong. I just wanted to say I think *Mamm* needs for you to move slowly. Holding hands with Andy so soon, she may think he's a rebound."

Charity was a rigid board. "You see me as immoral. Well, I told Andy about my miscarriage. He doesn't judge."

Her tone was so sharp. "Sister, I don't judge at all. This is something you're inflicting on yourself."

Tears spiked her lashes. "Really? If I said Andy wants me to stay out here to court, what would you think?"

I wanted to laugh, knowing how impulsive Andy was. But Charity was a real prize. "Well, you need to move slow. I learned that over the summer. Sometimes nothing seems clear. It's like walking in a haze. You know it got so dry here and so hot, the air seemed to blur images further away. Some folks here have never seen such a thing. But when you get up close, of course you can see. I didn't know my heart until the summer went on. Take things very slow with Andy. You can write. Nathan and I wrote, *jah?*"

Charity regained her confidence. "If Andy is for me, he can write and visit. *Mamm's* much better, but still not the same. *Grossdaddi's* idea of her living on a farm again shocked us all. *Mamm* does better on a farm, not the store."

"Well, she did it for Jeremiah. I give her credit."

Charity was pensive. Something else was on her mind. "What is it?"

"The store. Paul still comes in. Jeremiah tried to find another vendor for soda and candy but hasn't found one yet. I don't want to go back."

I reached for her hand. "You decide. Talk to *Mamm*. Things will become clear. And who knows? Maybe land will be found today and you'll be living here right quick."

Violet burst open the screen door. "*Daed's* here! Daisy's here!"

~*~

Daisy ran to Nathan and Violet, but their bandages shocked her and she ran back to me, hiding her head in my apron. Nathan called for her, but Violet asked him to take off the bandages first. Then Nathan reminded her of a time when she bruised her knee and the need to keep band-aids on. She calmed a tad and gingerly walked to them.

"I don't know where I can hug? Where do you hurt?"

Nathan knelt down. "A hug from you never hurts."

Daisy flew into his arms and he grimaced, but kissed her and gave her words of comfort. Violet told her that she'd hug her later, pointing to her bandaged arm.

Nathan urged the girls to go into the kitchen to see Aunt Naomi. He said he smelt cookies. They were quick to obey and Nathan opened his arms to me. "A hug from you never hurt either. And my lips are fine."

My heart swelled. I ran to him and he leaned down to give me the tenderest of kisses. He wrapped his good arm around me and I was at home. No matter where my family settled, wherever this man was, I was at home in his arms.

Giggling broke the romance. Violet and Daisy stood in the doorway, smiles wide. They asked if I would be there *mamm*, and I said yes. Oh, yes!

Discussion Guide

Dear Readers,

Thank you, as always, for choosing to read my books. There a so many *wunderbar gut* authors to choose from, and time is precious. Thank you for entering the 'little slice of heaven' I seek to create; the Amish of Smicksburg and Punxsutawney inspire me to no end!

While writing this book, I took my first weekend trip to Holmes County, Ohio. It's only a three hour drive, but I was just too hooked on Smicksburg to research and befriend other Amish communities. In Holmes County I met a horse and buggy Amish man who simply wants to be called Modern Amish. He said the group in is its infancy stage, so they don't have a name yet. Many Amish groups are named after the surname of the leader, hence you have Troyer Amish, Dan Weaver Amish, Beachy Amish, and so on. So, the mention of Modern Amish came from this man.

Let's call this man Freeman, as many Amish like to remain anonymous. He gave me his cell phone number! I could have fainted. He likes to talk and said I could learn so much more if we could have a nice, long talk on the phone. Usually, the Amish talk briefly on phones for business, not socialize. You're probably thinking he was a young man. No, he looked to be mid-sixties. Freeman said there are so many changes due to the technology boom, but he'll keep his horse and buggy. "It slows life down," he said.

My daughter asked me the other day if the Amish are dying out. If the Old Order "Real Amish", as she put it, will fade away. I gasped literally. *Ach, nee!* There's as many Amish as there are flavors of ice cream. The Amish grew by 100,000 over the past decade, according to an article in *Amish America*. Go over to their website for a wealth of information.

The biggest shock in the Amish world is the blur between Amish and Mennonite. Ten years ago, most Amish had little in common with Mennonites, but now there's a coming together of many. They want to be called Amish Mennonite. In *Spring Seeds*, the second book in this series, I have the Punxsutawney Amish Settlement connect more with local Mennonites. This is true, while the Amish of Smicksburg stand fast to their no cell phone rule.

1. With so many varieties of Amish, do you think you could be Modern Amish? With no shunning, the choice to drive cars, many modern appliances permitted, how different would your life be?

2. Out of all the characters in the book, who would you most want to be like and why?

3. Do you think Joy takes her vow to the Amish church too seriously or do you admire her?

4. Aunt Naomi has chased after hope. *Ach*, I love

this woman. Not having her own children, she can see the hand of God bringing others to her table, sharing life like kin. Do you lack community? Is there an Aunt Naomi to adopt?

5.   Aunt Abigail's death is the breaking point for the three families who want to leave the Amish. Have you ever had a tipping point in your life? How did you get through it? Were you stronger afterwards?

6.   If you were in Joy's shoes and you had to pick between David Mast or Nathan Good, what good character traits could you list for these men? Any red flags for either of these men?

7.   Joy takes walks to calm her spirit. 'Soul Care' is the new buzzword among Christians. In my opinion, not only do our souls need Bible reading, prayer and time for reflection, but hobbies. Fabric arts, especially knitting and crocheting calm me. I also enjoy reading British Classics. How about you? How can you have a whole soul?

8.   What is your opinion of Lily Mast after all that was discovered at the reconciliation dinner?

Did you judge her wrongly or should she have tried to get her husband help long ago? Did she depend too much on David?

9. If you were to have a cup of coffee with Charity, what advice would you give her? Should she rush into a relationship with Andy Weaver, or is this young man an answer to her prayers?

Naomi's Strawberry Pie

Pie Crust (Lazy Wife Pie Crust)

1 c. flour

3 Tbsp. powdered sugar

½ cup butter

Mix ingredients to make crumbs. Press into pie pan. Bake at 400 degrees for 20 minutes.

Strawberry Pie Filling

1 c. sugar

1 c. water

2 Tbsp. cornstarch (heaping)

2 Tbsp. white corn syrup

3 Tbsp. Strawberry Jell-O

1 ½ c. sliced strawberries

Cook until thick the sugar, water, cornstarch and corn syrup. Remove from heat, add Jell-O and strawberries. Let cool. Place in cooled pie crust. Top with Cool Whip if desired.

Uncle Micah's Root Beer

2 c. white sugar

1 gallon lukewarm water

4 tsp. root beer extract

1 tsp. yeast

Mix all ingredients together. Put in glass jars and cover. Set in sun for 4 hours. Refrigerate overnight.

About Author Karen Anna Vogel

Karen Anna Vogel is dusting off book outlines written thirty years ago when she was running after her four preschoolers. Having empty nest syndrome, she delved into writing. Many books and novellas later, she's passionate about portraying the Amish and small-town life in a realistic way. Being a "Trusted English Friend" to Amish in rural Western Pennsylvania and New York, she writes what she's experienced, many novels based on true stories. She also blogs at *Amish Crossings*

She's a graduate of Seton Hill University, majoring in Psychology & Elementary Education, and Andersonville Theological Seminary with a Masters in Biblical Counseling. Karen's a yarn hoarder not in therapy, knitting or crocheting something at all times. This passion leaks into her books along with hobby farming and her love of dogs. Her husband of thirty-seven years is responsible for turning her into a content country bumpkin.

Visit her at www.karenannavogel.com/contact

Karen's booklist so far (2018)
Check her Amazon author page for updates.

Continuing Series:
Amish Knitting Circle: Smicksburg Tales 1
Amish Knitting Circle: Smicksburg Tales 2
Amish Knit Lit Circle: Smicksburg Tales 3
Amish Knit & Stitch Circle: Smicksburg Tales 4
Amish Knit & Crochet Circle: Smicksburg 5

Standalone Novels:

Knit Together: Amish Knitting Novel
The Amish Doll: Amish Knitting Novel
Plain Jane: A Punxsutawney Amish Novel
Amish Herb Shop Series:
Herbalist's Daughter Trilogy
Herbalist's Son Trilogy
At Home in Pennsylvania Amish Country Series:
Winter Wheat
Spring Seeds
Summer Haze
Autumn Grace (Yet to be released)
Novellas:
Amish Knitting Circle Christmas: Granny & Jeb's Love Story
Amish Pen Pals: Rachael's Confession
Christmas Union: Quaker Abolitionist of Chester County, PA
Love Came Down at Christmas
Love Came Down at Christmas 2
Love Came Down at Christmas 3
Non-fiction:
31 Days to a Simple Life the Amish Way
A Simple Christmas the Amish Way

How to Know the Love of God

God so loved the world, that He gave His only Son, that whoever believes in Him should not perish but have eternal life. *John 3:16*

God so loved the world

God loves you!

"I have loved you with an everlasting love." — Jeremiah 31:3
"Indeed the very hairs of your head are numbered." — Luke 12:7

That He gave His only Son
Who is God's son?

"Jesus answered, 'I am the way and the truth and the life. No one comes to the Father except through me.'" — John 14:6

That whoever believes in Him

Whosoever? Even me?

No matter what you've done, God will receive you into His family. He will change you, so come as you are.

"I am the Lord, the God of all mankind. Is anything too hard   for   me?" — Jeremiah 32:27

"The Spirit of the Lord will come upon you in power, … and you will be changed into a different person." — 1 Samuel 10:6

Should not perish but have eternal life

Can I have that "blessed hope" of spending eternity with God?

"I write these things to you who believe in the name of Son of God so that you may know that you have eternal life." - 1 John 5:13

To know Jesus, come as you are and humbly admit you're a sinner. A sinner is someone who has missed the target of God's perfect holiness. I think we all qualify to be sinners. Open the door of your heart and let Christ in. He'll cleanse you from all sins. He says he stands at the door of your heart and knocks. Let Him in. Talk to Jesus like a friend…because when you open the door of your heart, you have a friend eager to come inside.

Bless you!
If you have any questions, contact Karen at www.karenannavogel.com

Summer Haze

www.ingramcontent.com/pod-product-compliance
Lightning Source LLC
Chambersburg PA
CBHW070618130626
46556CB00001B/408